"So you're not shy?"

A wicked smile curved Vito's lips.

"Definitely not. I just don't like to jump into anything without weighing the situation carefully," Christine answered.

"Good. Then you won't mind if I do this." With a flick of his finger, her sundress lay in a rumpled pile at her feet. She stood before him clad only in her blue bikini bottoms and matching strapless bra.

His bold gaze raked over her, making her ache for his hands to follow the same path.

"A very good trick, Mr. Cesare." She backed closer to the shower-stall door. "Is that what you learn over the course of seducing countless women around the globe?"

"Hardly." He reached for his belt buckle and whipped the length of leather out of the loops. "That's a trick I was only just inspired enough to try. Don't underestimate the appeal of seeing you naked."

Oh, he was good. Sexy as hell. Her gaze moved to his hand as he lowered his zipper. She licked her lips, her mouth suddenly too dry.

"I can see the appeal of naked," she agreed.

Dear Reader,

If you haven't guessed it already, I love writing about men who love sports. That makes sense, since I'm married to one—my husband spent the first ten years of our marriage as a sports editor. During that time I heard a lot about batting averages, NFL draft picks and shots on goal. None of which I find particularly exciting, but I enjoy seeing men get fired up about them. There's something about the male competitive drive that makes my pulse pound!

So it is with this hero, Formula One race car driver Vito Cesare. Vito's been in Europe for the past six years. Now he's back in Florida to prepare for his sister's wedding, but he wasn't expecting to find a green-thumb goddess tooling around his yard with a rake and making herself very much at home.

And of course, Christine Chandler has little use for jet-setting bachelor types when her whole life revolves around planting. I hope you enjoy the sparks when these two get together. Please visit me at www.JoanneRock.com to learn more about my future releases!

Happy reading,

Joanne Rock

Books by Joanne Rock

HARLEQUIN TEMPTATION
863—LEARNING CURVES
897—TALL, DARK AND DARING
919—REVEALED
951—ONE NAUGHTY NIGHT*

HARLEQUIN HISTORICALS
694—THE WEDDING KNIGHT

HARLEQUIN BLAZE
 26—SILK, LACE & VIDEOTAPE
 48—IN HOT PURSUIT
 54—WILD AND WILLING
 87—WILD AND WICKED
104—SEX & THE SINGLE GIRL*
108—GIRL'S GUIDE TO
         HUNTING & KISSING*
135—GIRL GONE WILD
139—DATE WITH A DIVA

*Single in South Beach

JOANNE ROCK

HER FINAL FLING

TORONTO • NEW YORK • LONDON
AMSTERDAM • PARIS • SYDNEY • HAMBURG
STOCKHOLM • ATHENS • TOKYO • MILAN • MADRID
PRAGUE • WARSAW • BUDAPEST • AUCKLAND

For Catherine Mann, my fearless critique partner and
wonderful friend who consistently pretends it's a pleasure to read
my work, even when it's two days before Christmas,
the day before out-of-town company arrives, or when she's
swamped with her own deadlines. Cathy, please know
you have my overwhelming and endless appreciation!

ISBN 0-373-69183-1

HER FINAL FLING

Copyright © 2004 by Joanne Rock.

This edition published by arrangement with Harlequin Books S.A.

® and TM are trademarks of the publisher. Trademarks indicated with
® are registered in the United States Patent and Trademark Office, the
Canadian Trade Marks Office and in other countries.

www.eHarlequin.com

Printed in U.S.A.

1

"PLEASE TAKE your hands *off* my fire bush." Christine Chandler stared down the man taking too many liberties with her delicate red petals.

Was the urge to manhandle somehow tattooed across the Y chromosome?

"Excuse me?" The sexy stranger dressed in a charcoal-gray suit with the jacket unbuttoned and tie undone slid his hand away from the dewy softness of the unfurling bud.

Sighing, Christine nudged past the man who'd appeared out of nowhere on the Miami property she was currently landscaping.

"The fire bush is very delicate and I can't afford to disturb the blooms before I transplant it." She swiped a wrist over her sweaty brow, wondering why she bothered when the man clearly had no business being out here in the sweltering Florida sun. But maybe he was just a nosy neighbor looking out for Mr. Donzinetti's property. The old Italian eccentric who'd hired her couldn't have been nicer, so it only made sense he'd have a few friends in the Coral Gables neighborhood. "I need to get back to work before my roots start to dry, but if you'd like to leave your name, I'll let the owner know you dropped by."

Christine smiled politely even though her mind was already taking silent inventory of the shrubs she still needed to plant along the rock facing of the sprawling, sixties-style ranch house. She didn't normally make time for too-handsome men wearing flashy gold watches and expensive sunglasses—even when she *didn't* look like the Swamp Thing reincarnated.

But she sure as heck wouldn't bother kowtowing to a guy whose suit probably cost more than her last month's rent now, when she had ten pounds of dirt under her fingernails. Where were her gloves when she needed them?

She just had to suffer his picture-perfect presence long enough to be sure she didn't offend one of Giuseppe Donzinetti's friends.

"You say you know the owner?" Mr. Armani sounded doubtful of the fact as he surveyed the property in the relentless heat of the southern Florida afternoon, then turned his sleek black Wayfarers toward her.

All five feet four filthy inches of her.

Well fine, if that's the way he wanted to play.

Shoving her dirt-covered trowel into an open loop on one leg of her cargo shorts, Christine used both hands to lift the large fire bush her uninvited guest had been examining when she discovered him. She hauled the shrub toward the new hole she'd just finished digging for her latest landscaping project.

The project that would make or break her fledgling landscape business. The same project that had such a tight deadline no other designer in town had been willing to touch it. Only someone as desperate as Christine would try to complete this total lot makeover in six weeks for a late summer wedding. At twenty-five, she might not have completed too many projects, but she was confident she could handle the Donzinetti property.

Edging around her unwelcome visitor, she resisted the urge to trail a muddy root across the fabric of his trousers. Would serve him right for getting in her way when she needed to be working her tail off today.

"Obviously I know the owner or I wouldn't be sweating like a pig to improve his property in the god-awful Miami summer heat." Okay, so maybe that came out a little testier than she'd intended, but for crying out loud. It's not like she was carrying a color TV out of the house. It had to be obvious to anyone—even a flashy Adonis whose eyes were hidden behind Oakley sunglasses. Those shades of his couldn't dim his vision that much, could they?

Settling the bush into the perimeter of a small garden designed to attract hummingbirds, Christine reminded herself not to be prejudiced against Mr. Pampered just because he reeked of wealth. No need to be biased because she had simple needs and simple values. And no cash.

"I'm sorry." He followed her, his dark leather shoes squashing through several yards of tilled ground to reach her. "I'm Vito Cesare and I happen to own this house jointly with my siblings."

Fingers faltering in the dirt she'd begun gathering around the fire bush, she peered back up at the man with a name straight out of *The Godfather*.

Taking in Vito's whipcord muscles that no amount of European tailoring could hide, she allowed herself a more careful inspection of her visitor. Dark brown hair grew too long around his face, while a neatly shaved patch of hair around his chin gave him a dissolute, Johnny Depp look. But his killer bod and custom-made suit belied the image.

"Like what you see?" He pulled off his shades and surprised her with keen hazel eyes instead of the brown she'd expected.

"Frankly, no. I was just thinking to myself that there isn't a chance in hell you're the owner's brother." Giuseppe Donzinetti had been dressed head-to-toe in clothes from the Gap. A neat, energetic little man, he'd talked with his hands as he'd ambled all over the sprawling Coral Gables yard to describe what he wanted her to accomplish.

"Who hired you? Was it Nico? Renzo? Marco? I know it couldn't have been my sister Giselle because I just talked to her a few days ago."

"Good Lord, how many of you are there?" Giving up her efforts to bury the shrub roots, she leaned back on her heels. "And I didn't contract with anyone named Cesare."

Suspicion mounting, she rose to her feet. "Which leads me to wonder what kind of line you're feeding me."

No man would ever trick her in a web of lies again. Least of all a guy named Vito who looked like trouble from the start. She'd been reeled in, hook, line and sinker, by a too-slick Internet Casanova last year who'd wooed her with poetry and promises before proposing online. She hadn't realized until she'd gotten an irate phone call from his *wife* that she was one of *eight* fiancées who'd been lured by his romantic lies.

Her BS detector was a hell of a lot more sensitive these days.

"I'm not feeding you any lines." Vito stuffed his sunglasses in the breast pocket of his shirt before wrenching off his jacket and then swiping a hand across his forehead. "And it's too damn hot to argue about this in ninety-nine-degree weather. Why don't you come inside where there's an air conditioner so we can sort this out?"

Over her dead body.

"Do you think I was born yesterday? I'm not going to let a total stranger into the house." Although, much to her happy fortune, she did possess a set of keys Mr. Donzinetti had loaned her as part of their deal. She'd given him the cut-rate bargain price he'd wanted and in return, he'd allowed her to stay on the property while her green thumb worked its magic.

Not only was the arrangement highly convenient for planting purposes, it had come at just the moment she'd realized she couldn't afford another month's rent on her shoe-box studio apartment.

"You don't need to let me in." He dug in his pants pocket and withdrew a well-worn key that appeared older and darker than the shiny bright gold one Mr. Donzinetti had cut for her. "I can get into my own house anytime I damn well choose."

Delving into her cargo shorts in search of her own key, Christine tried not to panic and failed. What if Mr. Donzinetti had just been a weird old man playing games with her and she'd never receive the rest of the payment on a job she'd been killing herself to complete? What if Giuseppe had Alzheimer's and had given her his neighbor's key instead of his own?

Finding what she sought, she dragged her key out of her pocket and held it up near his, hoping maybe Vito had the wrong damn key and he had been pulling her leg the whole time. Damned if they weren't mirror images of one another.

Please don't let this be happening.

"If you're really the owner, where have you been for the past week that I've been staying here? And for that matter, who is this Giuseppe Donzinetti character who hired me?"

"Uncle Giuseppe was here?" Vito unbuttoned another fastening on his shirt, drawing her eye to the deep bronze hue of the skin there, along with a sprinkling of black hair.

She fought the urge to tug at her collar, suddenly feeling the effects of the heat. But then his words hit home.

"He's a relative?" Maybe there was a chance her job here was still legit. That she'd be paid for all her hard work.

"A relative with no business bringing in guests without asking me, but yes, he's my uncle." He shoved up his shirtsleeves as a group of prepubescent boys whizzed past on the sidewalk, their skateboards bumping over every seam in the pavement. "Last I knew he was still in Naples. Italy, that is."

Oh, great. What if the weird old uncle with Alzheimer's had sailed back to Italy and left her here to contend with Vito's torn-up lawn and no payment in sight?

For the second time in her life, Christine Chandler found herself screwed by a situation that had looked too good to be true. Only this time, she had no one to blame but herself.

VITO CESARE had never been the kind of guy who picked fights with women.

And he definitely didn't want to upset the very dirty female who seemed to have single-handedly dug up fifty percent of his yard. For all he knew, she'd go plow up the rest if provoked.

But it was at least ninety-nine degrees outside his Coral Gables home, with enough humidity that he'd have to wring out his clothes by the time he got inside. Frankly, he was getting too cranky to discuss whatever the hell it was she was doing here while the sun deep-fried him on the front sidewalk. He'd just stepped off an international flight from Paris and he was fighting a bout of jet lag. Add to that the fact that he'd stayed up way too late the night before celebrating his latest racing win with an overenthusiastic female who'd had a really difficult time taking no for answer.

All of which meant he was operating on no sex, no sleep and no patience.

"Look. I'm sorry if there was a mix-up about the house, but I just had a twelve-hour flight and I'm going to lose it if I don't get a drink and cool down." He stalked toward his lone small suitcase the cab driver had left in the driveway as he shouted over his shoulder. "You're welcome to come in while we figure out this mess."

And he meant the "mess" part quite literally. His house was a bona fide disaster with all the old flower beds dug up, a tree cut down and lying in sawed-up chunks across the side yard and the cobblestone path to the front door piled into a heap of rubble. Just what in the hell did this woman who'd never bothered to introduce herself think she was doing to his property?

Strictly speaking, it wasn't all his. He really did own it in conjunction with his siblings since their father had died and left the family home to them all. But with his youngest brother at Harvard and determined to live up north, a soon-to-be married sister who already lived abroad and two other brothers who had bought houses with their significant others, Vito had begun thinking of the Cesare family home as his responsibility.

The way it had been for many years after their folks had died.

As the oldest of the Cesares, Vito had stepped in to raise his younger siblings. His mother had passed away in childbirth when he was barely a teenager, his father had followed her six years later. He'd taken care of the kids and the house until his sister was safely in college and his youngest brother was almost finished with high school. Then he'd given over the responsibilities to his brothers Nico and Renzo so he could finally live his own dreams on the European racing circuit.

The sound of footsteps on the driveway made him pause, pulling his head out of old memories. Turning as he reached the side door, he found the possessive owner of the fire bush on his heels, staring up at him with wary blue eyes.

"You can't go in," she informed him, tucking a strand of chin-length dark brown hair behind one ear. "The place is a little messy."

He peered around the yard and wondered if the inside could be as bad as the outside. Glancing back down at her dust-smeared khaki cargo shorts and damp gray T-shirt, he was hardly reassured. Although he'd be lying if he pretended not to notice the admirable curves beneath the layers of dirt. "How messy?"

"Considering you look like you just walked off a shoot for *GQ*, you'll probably think it looks pretty bad." She folded her arms under those admirable curves of hers and looked at him as though *he* was the one covered in grime. "But as far as I'm concerned, it's just all in a day's work."

That didn't sound good. At all. Vito's method of combating jet lag involved lots of sleeping, not cleaning. In fact, he'd grown accustomed to maid service since he'd traded surrogate parenthood to his younger siblings for life in the fast lane as a Formula One race-car driver. He hadn't picked up a mop in years.

And he didn't miss domestic duties one little bit.

Deciding that facing the mess couldn't be any worse than surviving the heat, Vito inserted his key in the lock.

Paused. Turned back to the woman behind him.

"I don't believe I caught your name."

"Christine Chandler. Sorry. I try to avoid introductions when my hands are dirty." She kept the hands in question tucked under her folded arms.

"Very understandable." Nudging open the door he stepped inside the kitchen of the sprawling ranch house his dad had bought when he moved to the U.S. Or at least, the room that used to be the kitchen.

Currently, the kitchen sink overflowed with flower cuttings, plant stems and mountains of dirt. The windowsill overlooking the backyard was crammed full of flower flats precariously balanced half on the sill and half on the dining-room chairs. Bags of potting soil and birdseed crowded the floor.

"Birdseed?" It was the least offensive question that sprang to mind when all he really wanted to know was what in the hell this insane woman was doing to his house.

His mother had always called their home "Hollywood tacky" with its open floor plan and sixties modern architecture. But it had felt like home to Vito with the big yard and tons of neighbor kids to grow up with. He always looked forward to coming home, but this time... Damn.

"For the birds," she explained very slowly as if only a complete moron would ask such an obvious question. Easing around the bags on the floor, she washed her hands over a tiny free corner of the sink. "Your uncle Giuseppe stressed that he hoped to attract a lot of birds."

"And you can't keep this stuff in the garage?"

"The birdseed, yes. I'll move it now that you're home." She nudged one of the bags with the toe of her work boot. "But I have to be careful with the plants because it's very hot in the garage and they'll stay fresher if I keep them cool. I can always move them out to the workshop."

Vito dropped his suitcase on top of a stack of empty flower flats by the door. Draping his jacket over the suitcase, he made his way to the refrigerator and hoped a drink would clear his head. He wanted straight scotch. He'd settle for a soda or anything else his brothers had left in the fridge.

He found only lemons. Tons and tons of lemons.

"I drink a lot of lemonade when I work." Drying her hands, she moved past him to grab a white pitcher off the door. Something he hadn't noticed thanks to the citrus garden growing on the other shelves. "Want me to pour you a glass while we discuss how to handle this miscommunication?"

He wasn't sure he even wanted to discuss it anymore. His whole world was in chaos and he'd been made a stranger in his own home.

Maybe he'd hunt down the scotch after all.

"Are you okay?" Christine stuffed a glass in one of his hands and then pried the open refrigerator door from his other. "I'd be happy to get out of your way and go back to work as soon as we establish that I am still getting paid for my efforts. I am going to get paid for all this, aren't I?"

She made a sweeping gesture to indicate his house, that ought to be condemned, and his eyesore of a yard that would piss off neighbors for miles around.

"Do you usually get paid for doing this?" He'd be surprised if she didn't get hauled off to jail. Was she exercising squatter's rights by moving into his house and making it hers?

He had to stifle an absurd urge to laugh as she seemed to genuinely consider his question.

"Honestly, sometimes I don't get paid because I'm very new at this, but I studied horticulture with the best landscape designers in California and now I'm ready to bring that knowledge to southern Florida." She busied herself by filling a paper cup with water and pouring the contents over the plants in his sink. "Your yard is my first large-scale production as a solo artist, but I've worked on bigger undertakings with other designers."

He leaned against the light wooden cupboards in the kitchen where he'd toasted his first Pop-Tart, weary with the way she seemed to talk in circles. For all he knew, his tired brain could be making it sound as though she was talking in circles when she was being perfectly rational.

"And just what did my uncle hire you to do here?" He made a mental note to call Giuseppe as soon as possible and ask him what the hell he thought he was doing jumping in to hire help for Vito without asking.

For that matter, why did Vito's whole family have to tiptoe around the fact that Vito was now a multimillionaire and could damn well afford to hire his own help? And his brothers were no better, paying to take care of every repair needed on the family home instead of letting him know when he needed to pitch in. According to Renzo and Nico, Vito had already given enough to the family coffers while they were growing up.

"I'm landscaping the property." She set down the paper cup and turned to face him, her back against the wine cabinet his brother Renzo had built long ago. "Your uncle said he wanted this place to be gorgeous by the time his niece's wedding rolls around, so I'm developing a large-scale overhaul." Pausing, she bit her lip, automatically drawing his gaze to that soft expanse of pink. "Do you know anything about this wedding, or is your uncle...you know...losing it?"

"He's not losing it." And even if he were, Vito would never let on as much to an outsider. He did wonder if Giuseppe really intended to pay Christine, or if he was leaving that up to Vito. He needed to discuss that matter with him when he called, too. "He probably wanted to surprise me. He didn't mention anything about me coming home while you were working?"

"Not so much as a whisper." She rearranged a length of ivy along a countertop, her hands treating the delicate vine with tenderness. "Believe me, I would have remembered that part."

No wonder she was a landscaper. She was obviously damn good with plants even if she didn't know squat about brooms or mops. Something about her gentle touch as she handled her foliage made him wonder...

He stopped himself cold, allowing her words to sink in. Could it be a coincidence that his uncle had hired a young woman who, Vito was beginning to realize, was actually very attractive underneath all that grass stain? And could it be random accident that Giuseppe had invited a woman to sleep in the house when he knew damn well Vito would be coming home for his sister's wedding?

Not a chance in hell.

"I'm afraid I have to apologize." Setting his empty lemonade glass on the counter, Vito thought he had a better handle on this whole bizarre situation now. Uncle Giuseppe, eternal matchmaker, strikes again.

"My uncle is a notorious family cupid and I have the feeling that he set us up to stumble on one another like this. Once he hired a pool boy for my aunt Lorraine who didn't even own a pool. Another time he wrote love poetry for his brother to help him land a woman. He takes a lot of joy putting people in one another's paths and seeing what happens. And since I'm way past marrying age in Uncle Giuseppe's book, I've apparently become his new target."

"Wait a minute." Christine frowned, her wide blue eyes turning a shade darker. Her shoulders straightened and her cheeks flushed pink. "Do you mean to imply your uncle only hired me as a potential hookup for you and not because of my landscaping skills?"

"Hell no." His uncle had been raised in a culture that didn't approve of hooking up. He approved of marriage. Kids. Family. But Vito wasn't about to share that with this gardening goddess who looked mad enough to spit nails. Although he had to admit that her pink cheeks were turning him on and making him think of wholly inappropriate other ways to make her flush like that. "He probably just wanted me to meet some more nice women—"

"I am not a *nice* woman." The female who'd been so gentle with her ivy plant and so protective of her fire bush looked ready to personally take him out if he dared to suggest otherwise. "And I will sue your uncle for breach of contract if he thinks he can pawn me off on some overgrown, flashy playboy who is so far removed from nature he wouldn't know what to do with a bag of birdseed if he tripped over it."

"Now wait a minute." Vito had always prided himself on having more patience than his hotheaded brothers who made a habit of speaking before thinking. But where did this woman get off calling him an overgrown playboy? And did she have any idea what it made a guy think when a woman told him she wasn't nice? "I don't think we need to start launching personal attacks to solve this. I was simply trying to share with you my uncle's motivations."

"Well you can tell him I don't appreciate being hired for my ass and not my professional assets, okay? I agreed to a job, not a blind date."

And before he could think of a comeback, Christine Chandler pivoted on her heel and walked right out the kitchen door.

If that didn't beat all.

Of course, Vito couldn't help moving to the kitchen window and watch the ass in question saunter away, hips twitching with her snappy walk down the driveway. He felt a little bad for enjoying the view and the residual sparks in the air when she was clearly mad, but hell, wasn't the urge to ogle tattooed across the Y chromosome?

Reaching for the door to follow her outside, hormones kicking to life, it occurred to him he didn't feel tired anymore.

2

CHRISTINE HATED to muck up her big exit by simply digging her hands right back in the dirt to continue working for a guy who saw her presence as pure fluff.

Then again, what choices did she have? Pausing in the middle of Vito Cesare's driveway, she scanned her brain for more options. Her beat-up secondhand truck was parked in the carport, so she possessed the means to leave. But where would she go?

She had no ready cash, and she was between apartments. Actually, she hadn't even thought about looking for a new apartment for another month since this job was supposed to have taken at least that long. And if she left now, she could kiss her dreams of owning her own landscaping business goodbye. If she went bankrupt, no one in their right mind would ever give her a loan to start up again.

Peering around the yard for inspiration, her gaze landed on the fire bush already wilting in the Florida heat. She couldn't just let the plant die so she could make a great exit.

Swallowing her pride, she trudged across the tilled up ground that would one day be a lush flower garden.

As she finished securing the bush into the ground and giving the shrub a nice long drink, she couldn't help but think of the fat investment account her older brother had started in her name.

She had the money to finance this dream. But damn it, she didn't want to start her own business with money someone else had earned. Her older brother Seth had worked long hours for years after their father walked out, slowly growing adept at reading the stock market and knowing where to invest. He'd made huge profits on his investments, funneling money to both Christine and their brother Jesse.

But she'd never been comfortable with the idea of someone else making money on her behalf. What kind of satisfaction would she take in owning her own business if the whole operation rode on the shoulders of Seth's hard work and not her own?

The answer remained the same as it had been for the last six months she'd struggled to start All Natural.

None.

Rinsing her hands in the stream from the hose before tossing aside the nozzle, Christine prepared herself to go back and face Vito Cesare. To somehow eat humble pie and pretend it tasted good.

Definitely not her forte.

But as she straightened, he was already there in front of her, dressed in olive-colored shorts and a white knit collared shirt. He held two glasses of lemonade in his hands.

He stepped over the hose to offer her a drink, his feet now visible in black flip-flops. "I would have come out sooner to apologize for that whole misunderstanding, but I thought it might be better if I cooled off first."

He looked far more approachable in flip-flops. The gold wristwatch was gone, as were the slick shades. She wholeheartedly approved of the more laid-back Vito. In fact, if she hadn't seen a glimpse of Vito the worldly jet-setter, she could almost be attracted to him.

Gulping down the lemonade he handed her, she decided she was the one who needed cooling off. No way would she develop a thing for the man who held the future of her fledgling business in his hands. Too unprofessional. Too tacky.

"Actually, I was just about to come looking for you to apologize, too." She pressed the bottom of her cool glass to her hot forehead, the icy cold condensation a welcome relief from the sultry temperature outdoors and her hot flashes inside. "I was sort of taken off guard to think your uncle didn't care about having the yard look really great. I wanted to be impressive with the best landscaping job I could provide and not because I look better in shorts than my competition, you know?"

His eyes flicked south at the mention of her legs and Christine found herself wondering how many other women had fallen victim to that hooded stare. Been there. Done that. Lived the public humiliation of having been taken in by a pro.

She swigged the rest of her drink and kept her mind on business.

"I understand better than you think." He nodded toward the house. "There are some chairs around back on the patio if you want to sit for a minute."

Nodding, she followed him since they obviously had a few glitches to iron out together.

"So, are you suggesting you know what it's like to be hired for your bod instead of your brains, Cesare?" She could hold her own with this guy as long as she kept things light, easy. She would put herself in the driver's seat of this relationship and stay there.

"As a matter of fact, I do. Sort of." He led them to the patio that she'd commandeered for peat moss.

Thankfully, she'd used all the bags of manure a week ago.

She couldn't picture Vito hanging out around the fertilizer, even in his flip-flop guise. Settling into the wrought-iron chair across from him with a big glass-topped umbrella table between them, she placed her empty glass on the surface and was grateful the lawn wasn't in full destruction mode back here. A tire swing still hung in an old banyan tree behind a big workshop in the backyard. "And how is it that you end up being judged on your looks? Are you an underwear model on the side?"

"Are you suggesting I'd have a future in the industry?"

"Just taking wild guesses." She wished she hadn't

emptied her glass so quickly as she conjured images of Vito in his underwear. Was he a boxers or briefs kind of guy?

Considering his flashy clothes earlier, she'd have to go with silk boxers. But if ever a man had been built for tighty-whiteys...

"Christine?"

Her underwear daydreams faded at Vito's voice. "Sorry. You were saying?"

"I'm a race-car driver." The humor in his eyes suggested he knew the direction of her daydreams. "And sometimes people bet on a driver because he looks good in his racing suit instead of how well he drives. That bugs me, too, so I don't blame you for being miffed that my uncle would be so superficial. If it makes you feel any better though, I'm sure he never would have hired you if he didn't think you'd do a great job on the landscaping. He's really excited about Giselle's wedding."

"You race cars?" Christine didn't know squat about any sport. For that matter, was racing even considered a sport since it didn't have a damn thing to do with being athletic?

"I'm a Formula One driver." At her blank look, he continued. "It's open-wheel racing. You know, as opposed to stock cars like NASCAR?"

"Don't have a clue about any of those, actually. Although I'm sure you look very cute in the racing suit." She'd flirt with him before he had the chance to flirt with her, putting herself firmly in control of the situation. No sense making herself seem like a novice when it came to men. She wouldn't be taken advantage of again. "But back to the matter at hand, what do you suggest we do in relation to my work here?"

He peered around the yard, his square shoulders settling deeper into the wrought-iron patio chair. "I think you'd better keep working. No offense, Christine, but it looks like a natural disaster around here."

"It's a work in progress." She wasn't always the neatest person, even when she wasn't involved in an extensive landscaping job. But she could see the potential for the yard and had every confidence it would be gorgeous by the time she finished. "Besides, I was operating under the impression that the house would be vacant except for me, so I'll admit I've been a little more lax about daily cleanup just because I'm working such long hours on this job. It doesn't make much sense for me to put away my tools in the garage every night when I'm only going to need them six hours later."

"You're putting in that much time on the yard?"

"Have you seen the property recently? It was in shambles. Not that it looked terrible from the street or anything, but from a professional perspective, it needed to be almost started from scratch. Just keeping up with all the watering is more than a full-time job for transplants in this heat." She leaned closer, elbows on the table. "But you think I'll be able to stay on here and finish up the job?"

She folded her hands inward so he wouldn't see her crossing her fingers.

"Definitely. I sure as hell couldn't have my baby sister come home with the house looking like this. Giuseppe told you it needs to be ready to go September first?"

"It won't be a problem as long as I can continue to work at manic speed, which means I can't take off many afternoons like this." She plucked her T-shirt away from her damp skin in the hope of catching a breeze. "And I'd also need to be able to stay onsite so I can maximize my work hours. Do you have any family you can stay with for a few weeks while I finish up? Giuseppe, maybe, since he's the one who assured me I'd have twenty-four-hour access to the property?"

"That could be a problem." Vito drained his lemonade glass with one long swallow. The upturned glass dripped condensation down into the open neck of his collared shirt, drawing Christine's eye to that dark expanse of skin glistening with a slight sheen.

She blinked fast before the underwear fantasy came back.

"How so? If you don't want to stay with your uncle, maybe you could stay at a swanky hotel while you're in town. Aren't European race-car drivers practically made of money?"

"No. But money isn't really the issue here—it's more of a comfort concern. I like to stay at the house whenever I'm in the States. I grew up here, so it's sort of...home." He met her gaze, his hazel eyes dark and intense despite his relaxed tone.

Christine had the feeling he wouldn't be changing his mind on the issue anytime soon.

"Well, we can't both stay here." What did he expect her to do—pitch a tent out front for the next month?

"Why can't we?"

For a moment she thought he really wanted her to get to work on the tent, until she realized she'd never said that part out loud. "You mean both of us in the house?"

"It housed a family of seven before my parents died. Later it accommodated five kids, most of them teenagers. I think it ought to be able to handle two of us." He grinned. "You don't look like you take up much room."

Did she understand this man correctly? "I'm sorry, I must be out of mind, because I could have sworn you suggested that I take it on blind faith you aren't some kind of psychopath and should share the house with a virtual stranger."

His grin faded. "You've got a point. If my sister pulled a stunt like that, I'd— Well let's just say I'd be mad and leave it at that."

"See? You making vague threats of hypothetical retribution isn't convincing me you're not a psychopath, that's for sure." Damn it, why did he have to show up today and throw a huge wrench in her plans? She needed this job, needed to work things out with him.

"If you could convince Giuseppe to foot the hotel bill

for me, I suppose I could make the trip back and forth. I just don't like to drive when I'm tired." And by the time she was done with the physically demanding work this job entailed, she was usually so bone-weary she was cross-eyed. What if she knocked herself out to make her business work, only to wrap her piece-of-junk truck around a telephone pole because she fell asleep at the wheel?

"No. You're working too hard already. Don't you have any other employees or co-workers who could help you out with this job?"

How could she afford to hire anyone when she could barely keep herself afloat? Of course, she wouldn't tell him that. "I'm giving your uncle a cut-rate price. There's no budget for anyone else."

"I can increase your budget." He looked ready to whip out a checkbook then and there.

And she definitely didn't want to get roped into that discussion.

"Look. I appreciate the offer, but I'm not trying to bleed more money from you. I just want to be able to fulfill my end of the bargain with your uncle." Was it her fault the guy had had more than gardening on his mind when he'd hired her?

"Okay. How about this—I'll haul a few neighbors over here to vouch for me. For that matter, you can have my license and check me out."

Vito had to admit he respected a woman who looked out for herself. How could he have suggested for a minute that she stay in the house with him when for all she knew he was a wanted man in ten states? She hadn't even recognized his name from his racing career, so she wouldn't know the first thing about him.

"What do I look like, a private eye? I don't want your license." She brushed aside the idea with an airy wave of her hand.

Vito studied her the way he'd check out a new race-course, seeking hidden obstacles and tricky angles. She was tougher than she looked with her wispy brown hair fluttering around her chin and her short stature. Despite her delicate features and heart-shaped face, she was a hard worker in a physically demanding job.

She was also pretty damn sarcastic.

"I realize you're not a private eye. Don't you have any friends who are cops? Or you could look up my name on the Internet and make sure there aren't any stories about me getting arrested or groping unsuspecting landscapers." Women couldn't be too careful these days. How many times had he told his sister Giselle that very same thing? "Do you have any family in the area? Anyone who can watch your back while you're out working?"

Who made sure she arrived home every day? In her line of work, she must meet a lot of strangers.

She frowned, those narrow arches of her eyebrows flattening into one line of dark scowl. "I imagine your job is far more dangerous than mine. And I certainly don't need my family to help me run my business."

Touchy subject, apparently. Vito made a mental note to revisit the topic at another time.

Wait a minute. Had he really just planned for future personal discussions with Christine Chandler, prickly gardener and owner of a very tempting pair of legs?

Bad idea, given his brief time in the States and his dating code of ethics. He made it a point not to get involved with women who weren't looking for the same things from a relationship as him. And he could almost guarantee that this woman who put down roots for a living wouldn't be romanced by the idea of a fast fling.

Time to rein in those wayward thoughts about her sexy legs and the enticing contrast between her nurturing profession and her tough personal side.

"So what do you suggest?" he asked, the oppressive heat robbing him of alternative ideas for their dilemma.

"The house is very big," she admitted. "And it's not like I spend all that much time in it."

Vito about fell out of his chair. She'd been driving such a hard bargain about the house issue. Was she actually relenting? No matter what she said to him about not trying to angle for money on this job, Vito would make sure Giuseppe gave her some sort of bonus for all her overtime hours and having to deal with the inconvenience of him showing up. That was only fair compensation.

But given her prickly independent nature, Vito would make certain any bonus looked like it came from Giuseppe and not from him.

"I've got a lot to do while I'm in town, too," he lied,

certain he'd find something to keep him occupied so that he didn't scare her off a job that was obviously very important to her. He had some game software he'd been trying to develop over the past few years.

Besides, despite the stern reminder to himself about the whole dating ethics thing, some deep-seated guy instinct reminded him that Christine was one of the most intriguing women he'd been around in a long time. After the artifice of too many Barbie-doll babes in his world, he couldn't help but appreciate the way Christine seemed so genuine. So real.

"Fine." She gave a brusque nod and rose to her feet, putting him at eye level with her hips. "How about we go see a few of your neighbors tonight. If they can vouch that you're really the owner of this place and—to their knowledge—a good guy, I'll get back to my work here and we'll just try to stay out of one another's way in the house."

Even the thrill of an open track couldn't compare to the unexpected adrenaline surge her declaration inspired. He'd probably slept in closer proximity to strangers in nearby hotel rooms than he would with Christine in the sprawling ranch house, but that didn't stop his adolescent excitement at the sleepover plans.

What if she exited the shower in just a towel? Or forgot to put on a robe when she prowled around the house for a midnight snack? The possibilities were endless. And Vito couldn't believe that all of those goofy scenarios inspired more interest than easy sex with the latest European model or South American heiress.

Working hard to keep the grin off his face, Vito rose to his feet and reminded himself he was a gentleman.

Damn it.

"It's a deal." He replaced the wrought-iron patio chairs and stepped around the mountain of bags containing the foreign-sounding substance named peat moss. Venturing closer to Christine, he extended his arm and told himself being a gentleman could be a good thing. For starters, it made him positive that his neighbors would have only great things to say about him.

"Why don't we go see Mrs. Kowolski first?" He pointed to the house next door, knowing damn well the widow who ran a catering business out of her home rarely left her kitchen. "I hope you're hungry because I've never once been to her house when she didn't force me to eat something."

Ignoring the arm he offered her, she jumped off the patio instead of taking the two low steps down. "Great. I'm starving."

Christine was already trekking across the rough patches of torn-up lawn in the direction he'd pointed, tanned calves flexing as she navigated the awkward terrain with ease. Vito followed her, reminding himself that American women were a whole different breed.

Independent. A little stubborn, maybe. And very, very sexy.

His appetite was definitely calling to him by now, and he didn't think Mary Jo Kowolski's cookies were going to do a damn thing to satisfy the hunger.

3

ENSCONCED in Mary Jo Kowolski's kitchen an hour later, Christine began to wonder if she would be able to finish transplanting the other fire bushes before the sun set. She'd somehow walked into a massive PR campaign for Vito since Mary Jo was launching into yet another tale of his youth as she refilled Christine's glass of raspberry tea.

"And then there was the time he organized the neighborhood go-cart drag race. Did he tell you about that, Christine?" Round-cheeked and smiling, Mary Jo had to be approaching sixty, but her bright red T-shirt reading Bloom Where You're Planted and her masterful organization of ten different things cooking in her ovens made her seem younger.

"Mrs. Kowolski, Christine and I hardly know each other," Vito reminded her, swiping a lemon cookie off a tray she'd just taken from the oven. He tossed the hot treat from hand to hand, a ritual Christine suspected was his method of helping it cool off. "We should probably be going so that Christine can—"

"Not one of the Cesare kids will call me Mary Jo to this day. Can you imagine? It makes me feel a hundred years old." Mary Jo waved hello out the kitchen window to an older lady walking a white terrier and then shoved a plate in front of Vito for his cookie. "Anyhow, Vito was always the quiet one compared to his brothers who can all talk your ear off."

Christine thought that was saying a lot since Mary Jo seemed fairly verbal herself.

"But he was serious about racing from the time he was knee-high to a grasshopper," she rattled on, moving like a whirlwind through the big country kitchen decorated with lots of cows and painted milk cans. "And when he was probably about twelve he posted flyers all around Coral Gables about his drag race. He charged an entry fee and used it to buy trophies. Even the local cops showed up to watch the race."

"Did he win?" Christine munched on her scallops wrapped in bacon and decided being a caterer beat landscaping hands down.

Sparing a glance for Vito who had been giving her apologetic smiles every few minutes, she noticed he was hanging his head.

"Oh, no." Mary Jo turned on a big electric mixer in one corner of the room and let it do its noisy job while she simply raised her voice to be heard over the racket. "He got beaten soundly by the Baker boys up the street, but the neighborhood kids loved the event so much they made it an annual thing for the next four years, and after that Vito never lost, did you, hon?" She reached over the kitchen island to pat Vito's cheek as if he was still ten years old, then turned her mixer back off. "It's good to have you home. And I'm so glad we've got a couple of months to work on keeping you here. I can't wait for your sister's wedding."

Vito slid off the tall chair perched at the kitchen island. "It's going to be great to have the family together again. I couldn't stay in town long after Renzo's wedding this spring, so it will be nice to have more time to see friends this trip."

Christine finished her tea and licked her lips as she rose, wondering if she could find an excuse to drop in on Mary Jo again. The food she normally ate on her work break was more in the peanut-butter-and-jelly vein.

Moving the lemon cookies to a cooling rack with the smooth efficiency of a seasoned pro, Mary Jo winked at Vito. "I can't wait to meet the man you finally deemed good enough for your little sister. Did you tell your friend Christine about the time you followed Giselle to her prom and then hid in the bushes when she went parking with her date?"

"That story got really blown out of proportion." Vito backed toward the door as if to flee, but Christine thought she had time for a final Vito story.

She remained rooted to the spot.

"Apparently he neglected to tell me that one. Can you possibly spare another cookie, Mary Jo?" Even after the plateful of scallops, she was dying for a sweet. And the kitchen smelled so lemony good.

"I always have plenty," she insisted, dealing out another red ceramic plate and three cookies faster than a Vegas card sharp. "In fact I'll pack up a box for you to take home while I tell you about poor Giselle's prom night."

Christine snagged one of the warm cookies while Vito groaned behind her. She was finding it increasingly difficult to reconcile her initial impression of him as Mr. Flashy in his European suit and expensive gold watch with the same person Mary Jo Kowolski kept talking about.

"Well, none of the Cesare boys liked anyone to date their sister. I can't tell you how many young men I saw approach their house once Giselle turned sixteen, but those brothers sent all of them away because none of them was good enough for her as far as they were concerned."

"Mrs. K., that's not totally true—"

Mary Jo shook a finger at Vito and smiled. "You had your chance to share the story, but you didn't. Now it's my turn."

Christine wondered if anyone ever got a word in edgewise around Mrs. Kowolski.

"Anyhow, we were all surprised when Billy Spears asked Giselle to the prom and she said yes. I had my doubts about whether or not Giselle would actually make it out of the house that night, but sure enough, I saw her leave just as I was putting the finishing touches on a friend's wedding cake."

Christine understood all too well how difficult it could be to have overprotective older brothers breathing down your neck. She'd grown up with two brothers determined to keep her safe, especially after their father walked out, which meant they usually scared off all prospective boyfriends.

No wonder she found herself rooting for Giselle and Billy.

"And then, what do I see out my kitchen window?" Mary Jo pointed with a thumb over her shoulder to her view of the sidewalk and the Cesares side yard. She removed a huge silver bowl from underneath the electric mixer and moved it to another counter where she'd set out her cookie sheets. "Huey, Dewey and Louie, better known as Vito, Nico and Renzo, all pile into the family car to follow them."

"We were going to a party," Vito interjected. "Both Marco and Giselle had gone out, so we felt entitled to a night on the town, too. We weren't following my sister."

Mary Jo gave him a brush-off smile as if she didn't believe a word. "Still, Vito and his brothers came back a few minutes after Giselle pulled into the driveway with her date and—"

"We knew when she was supposed to be home and we were running late," Vito explained, cramming his words in on top of Mary Jo's.

She paused in the process of dabbing globs of cookie dough on the baking sheets. "And when he found his little sister necking in the car, he probably took ten years off Billy's life by personally hauling him out of the vehicle."

Vito shook his head as if still disgusted with the incident that was probably nearly a decade old. "The punk was all over my sixteen-year-old sister and gunning for first base—in *my* driveway, no less. I was damn proud I handled the matter with no bloodshed."

Thinking she'd probably tormented Vito enough with this walk down memory lane, Christine scooped up the box of cookies and drifted closer to the door. "In other words he took the whole protector thing pretty seriously?"

Mary Jo winked. "I think he still does."

Vito was already outside holding the door for Christine.

She hoped he didn't think she needed any chivalry. She'd left home the moment she turned eighteen just so she could be her own person and make her own mistakes.

Which, of course, she'd done in spectacular fashion. She'd thought she was being so smart and conservative by getting to know Rafe online before she let herself get swept away by his sensitive notes and romantic poems. At least she hadn't jumped straight into bed with him, right?

Ha! She would have been a lot better off having a fling than getting engaged to a man who already had a wife and had lined up seven other sucker fiancées.

"Thanks for the cookies, Mrs. K." she called, stepping outside into the Florida twilight.

"Nice meeting you, hon," the woman hollered back as the screen door slammed. "Come back anytime!"

"Sorry about that." Vito paused when they reached the street. "I didn't mean to spend so long at her house, but she's a really nice lady even if she likes to trot out all my secrets."

"I bet that's not all your secrets." Christine savored the marginally cooler air now that the sun was setting. If she hadn't known better, this time spent with Vito could almost feel like a date. Good thing she wasn't such a starry-eyed romantic anymore, right? "I'll wager your lifestyle abroad is a far sight more colorful—and secret—than your life over here."

God, that sounded like a come-on. Giving herself a mental shake and a stern reminder of where fanciful thoughts had led her the last time, Christine decided to make tracks back to her sweaty physical labor before she started thinking about other ways of getting sweaty and physical with the undeniably delicious Vito.

Turning her gaze back to the torn-up Cesare yard, she promised herself she'd ditch Vito and all thoughts of a sexy interlude ASAP.

VITO STARED DOWN at Christine in the rosy light of sunset and wondered how many more neighbors' ancient stories he'd have to suffer through before he could go home.

With her.

"I refuse to answer that until you tell me something about you." In fact, he wasn't budging until he knew more about this woman full of contrasts. Her pixie figure versus her very healthy appetite was the most recent of his intriguing discoveries about her. "You know all the dirt on me now, but I don't know the first thing about you other than you run your own business and you don't like anyone to handle your petals too roughly."

He didn't know what demon within made him add in that last part. He had the feeling he shouldn't be flirting with her if he wanted to convince her they could successfully share the same house for the next six weeks.

But she didn't blush or look the least bit flustered. Instead, she jammed her box of cookies under one arm and faced him head-on. All business.

"Fair enough. I'm a Tampa native but I went to college in L.A. I wanted to put as much distance between me and the overbearing men in my family. But now I'm back in the same state as my older brothers and I'm determined to develop my own business independent of anyone's help—financial or otherwise."

Was it his imagination, or did he detect a note of warning in her voice? And how had she come to be so damn prickly at such a young age? She couldn't be much older than twenty-five.

She waved to a little girl pushing her way down the sidewalk on a scooter before she took up her story again. "My five-year plan sees All Natural thriving as an independent success while my ten-year goals include opening offices in other Florida cities. Either that, or I might just open a nursery of specialty plants you can't find anywhere else. I don't date much because I work too hard and I spend the majority of my waking hours with dirt under my fingernails."

He found it interesting she opted to slide in her dating stance. Another warning, no doubt.

"Just out of curiosity's sake, are men in the five-year plan?" Not that he was jockeying for position or anything.

"Men aren't even in the long-term planning unless I get really lonely. And even then... Well let's just say I don't need much in that department to tide me over." Glancing around the neighborhood, she peered back at Vito's ranch house. "And I think that bit of sharing probably evens up the score don't you? I really need to do a few more things around the yard before it gets totally dark."

Letting her off the hook for now, Vito definitely planned to ask her about her opposition to dating sometime down the road. Her stance surprised him since he had her pegged for more the home-and-hearth type with her green thumb and nurturing career.

But he had to admit, her anti-relationship views opened up some very intriguing possibilities for them this summer.

"Don't you want to go talk to a few more neighbors?"

Vito had seen Mrs. Hollenbeck walking her dog on the street earlier. She'd vouch for him in a heartbeat, assuming she'd forgiven him for feeding Fluffy pizza the one and only time he'd done any dog-sitting. How was he supposed to know Fluffy had wheat allergies?

"Are you kidding? I just got your whole life story from Mary Jo." Christine hurried back over to his yard, her low-cut work boots moving silently over the dark ground, her hair fluttering around her chin with the help of a welcome breeze. "I'm confident there's not a chance you could be a homicidal maniac without her knowing all the details. Even if you did have a dark and wicked side, I'm sure you wouldn't want to exercise it for fear of jeopardizing lifetime access to the best cookies in southern Florida."

Setting her box of sweets on the tailgate of the rusty pickup truck parked under the carport, she circled around to retrieve a few tools still lying around the property.

Vito ducked into the carport to turn on a couple of floodlights and then followed her across the yard, enjoying the view from behind. "The people around here are pretty nice. They were all really good to the family after our folks died. Mrs. Kowolski fed us for a week before Giselle decided she wanted to take up cooking. Nico grew pretty talented in the kitchen, too, but me and Renzo—forget it. We would have been living on Cap'n Crunch without some help."

Giselle's exploits as a superstar chef were a welcome

topic of conversation normally, but Vito didn't want to overload his guest on his first day back in town. She probably knew more than she ever wanted to know about the Cesares.

"How can I help?" He took a shovel from her since she was juggling too many tools.

"I don't need any help." She smiled brightly before trudging to an outbuilding at the back of the property that his brother had built for his woodworking. "And I can get the shovel, too, so please don't feel like you need to stick around if you have other things to do. I'll probably be busy for a few more hours at least."

"Aren't you picking up for the night?" Somehow he'd had visions of them going inside together. Talking. Hanging out. Hell, he didn't know what he had in mind.

He knew perfectly well it was too soon to act on this attraction to Christine.

"No, I'm just organizing so that my work space doesn't look like a disaster area now that you're here. I'll clean up in the house before I go to bed, too, and I'm sorry about all the plants in the sink. I can guarantee they're bug-free, however."

Damn, he hadn't even thought about the infestation potential.

"It's not a problem." Especially since he always had someone come in to clean the house whenever he was in town. What was the point of all his racing winnings if he couldn't occasionally dip into them for a few perks?

After having struggled and scrimped to help his brothers and Giselle pay for college, who could blame him for a little self-indulgence now? "And damn it, Christine, let me give you a hand just for tonight since I threw off your whole workday by showing up."

Ducking into the workshop, Christine switched on a lamp. Of course, this being his brother's old carpentry haven, the lighting wasn't just a bare electric light bulb. Although the rest of the room had been cleared out of hand carved desks and elaborate sideboards, the over-size shed still boasted wooden wall sconces at three-foot intervals.

Just what every backyard storage shed needed.

With a thunk, Christine set down the tools she'd been lugging on the sealed concrete floor.

"Look. I don't mean to be rude, Vito, and I've had a surprisingly nice day hanging out with you, considering you're some sort of European playboy extraordinaire. But I have a really hard time accepting help and I feel a big sense of ownership on this project, so if you don't mind..."

"You want me to leave you alone." He set down his shovel, the only tool she'd let him carry. She'd given him loud and clear warnings about the whole independence thing, so he wasn't surprised there. But he was surprised to feel a twinge of disappointment. "Fair enough. I just wanted to make sure things were cool between us before I went inside."

"They're very cool." She straightened the tools in the corner of the half-empty shed and failed to meet his eye.

Too bad he didn't feel very cool at the moment. Watching her walk all over the yard, her slender hips in constant motion, had produced quite the opposite effect.

"Good." He didn't mean to move closer to her, but somehow he had. Just for a moment. "Because I wouldn't want things to be awkward for you, having to sleep under the same roof as me."

She blinked up at him, their bodies suddenly too close together, the pink bow of her mouth forming a round O of slight surprise.

He thought about taking that mouth, about tasting the lemony sugar of her kiss and putting an end to the mix of awkwardness and attraction between them. But given all her boundary-drawing and warning signs posted, Vito thought maybe he'd be better off letting her go this time. Saving that kiss for a moment when neither of them would find any reason to stop.

"'Night, Christine." Easing away from her and the raw temptation of her tanned, slender body, Vito took a step back. Her boundaries were safe for a little while longer. "Pleasant dreams."

And for the first time in a long time, he knew damn well that his would be.

4

TWO WEEKS LATER, Christine was still cursing Vito Cesare's insistence that she have pleasant dreams.

Slumping into the ancient tire swing in the backyard after another endless day of working, she stared up at the dark house where Vito worked on his computer and wished she could get a good night's sleep for a change. But she'd been having so many confounded pleasant dreams of him that she dreaded going to bed lately for fear of the overly romantic plotting of her subconscious mind.

Wrapping her arms around the old tire, she rested her chin on her hands and kicked the swing into motion, every muscle aching from spending her day on her hands and knees finishing the hard-scaping, or structural work for the new landscape. She'd installed new patio blocks and pathways around the property, creating all new foundations and focal points for the colorful tropical gardens she had yet to develop.

But despite her bone-weary exhaustion, she couldn't help but fantasize about the man she'd shared a house with for the last two weeks. He'd been a perfect gentleman ever since that first night when he'd helped her put away the tools in the workshop. She'd been taken aback by his sudden proximity that night, and could have sworn he'd been about to kiss her. And then...nothing.

A reminder to have pleasant dreams, and then he was off to his own room, staying out of her way day after day while she worked sunup to well after sundown creating the kind of lush foliage and private terrain she and Giuseppe Donzinetti had discussed.

She'd made it her habit to work late every night. Not only because she needed to get a lot done, but also because she hoped she'd dream about him less often if she didn't run into him in the hallway before going to bed. She opted to clean up in the charming outdoor shower she'd found behind the outbuilding at the back of the property instead. An adorable latticework enclosure complete with wooden privacy screens, the shower stall had to have been built by the Cesare brother who had been into carpentry.

Not only did she avoid Vito that way, but she really enjoyed showering under the stars, sliding into some clean clothes, and then sneaking into the house after Vito was asleep. But tonight she was too exhausted even to make it back to her bed.

A warm evening breeze fluttered through her damp hair as she studied the dark house for some sign of life. It was only midnight and she'd noticed Vito sometimes stayed up until one or two. He left the house for long periods of time during the day, coming home at seven or eight and offering her dinner most nights.

Which she had always refused. Except for earlier in the week when he'd simply brought bags of takeout home and set them on the picnic table for her. Considering his idea of takeout had been Cajun-fried shrimp and jambalaya from a local specialty restaurant, she could hardly have refused. But even then, he'd left her alone to eat in peace.

Which had been very gentlemanly. And, if she was completely honest with herself, maybe just a teeny bit disappointing.

Had she dreamed the mutual attraction of that first day? Or had the chemistry between them been so one-sided it had skewed her perceptions?

Yawning and stretching, she told herself to quit ruminating and just get her butt inside so she could snag some sleep. Then again, maybe if she closed her eyes out here, farther away from where Vito slept, she'd be able to catch a few Zs that weren't interrupted by sultry dreams. Surely even her romantic subconscious wouldn't plague her with sexy visions while she was perched in a ring of vulcanized rubber.

After two weeks, maybe she'd found the key to a few hours of sleep that didn't star Vito Cesare wearing nothing but a pair of gardening gloves and a wicked grin.

FEET SINKING into the soft earth beneath his flip-flops, Vito walked across the yard at 2:00 a.m. to find Christine slumped in the old tire swing, her chin resting on her folded hands. He paused over her, wondering what she was dreaming about. He'd wake her in a minute and steer her to bed so she could get a good night's sleep. For now he simply indulged in the unique experience of watching her at rest.

Did she think about fire bushes and patio blocks even while she slept? Plants and landscaping seemed to be all she talked about while awake. The few times he'd tried to draw her into conversation over the last two weeks that he'd been back home, she'd quickly rerouted the discussion back to watering schedules and his yard's soil composition.

All business, in other words.

He studied her face in the moonlight. Swiping a thumb across her cheek, he told himself he was just brushing off a stray hair and not testing the softness of her creamy skin. Although if he *had* been taking note of what she felt like, he would have had to admit her skin was even softer than he'd imagined. More delicate.

Debating the best way to wake her, Vito skimmed a short brown lock of hair away from her face, exposing the full expanse of her cheek to the moonbeams, along with her tempting pink lips.

He'd been trying to give her space ever since that first night when she'd outlined her boundaries as concretely as if she'd laid her damn paver stones around them. He'd hoped that maybe with time and enforced proximity, the spark between them would develop into something even she couldn't ignore. But she was either too exhausted to look at him twice or she deliberately avoided him. He couldn't be sure which.

And since the out-of-town guests would start arriving for the wedding preliminaries in another week or so, Vito knew he didn't have much more time to make his move. If he wanted to woo Christine, he couldn't afford to sit back and wait for her boundaries to dissolve any longer.

Tomorrow, he'd pick up his pace for the full-throttle rush toward the finish line and break through those barriers of hers on his own. Tonight, he'd have to settle for cruising one more test lap.

"Christine?" He laid his hand on her shoulder, debating if he should just scoop her out of the swing and carry her to bed. She had to be dead to the world after all the hours she'd been putting in this week.

Then again, he didn't want to risk scaring her.

"Christine?" he called her name a little louder, looping an arm around her waist to test her reaction.

"Vi-to." She moaned his name in her sleep, stretching out the word into extra syllables as if savoring the taste of it on her tongue.

His name had never sounded more provocative. And although she still seemed to sleep deeply, with her chin resting on the back of her hand curved around the tire, Vito suddenly felt very, very awake.

Damn.

Unwilling to torment himself any longer, he simply scooped her up out of the swing and into his arms. Her head lolled against his shoulder like a rag doll's, her arms wrapping reflexively around his neck. Her whole body seemed to sigh against his, her hip curved alongside his waist while her breast molded sweetly to his chest.

As his body responded instantly to hers, he couldn't decide if carrying her had been a great idea or a really stupid one. She might sleep better tonight after he laid her in her bed, but he knew damn well his night wouldn't exactly be restful.

Toeing open the French doors that led to the dining room, Vito brought her through the darkened house to his brother Nico's old bedroom. Now that Nico was engaged to the CEO of the hottest resort on South Beach, the former NHL star lived on Palm Island with his soon-to-be wife. The room still bore a few of his old hockey posters and a signed puck from the first professional game he'd ever attended, but other than that, the room was purely Christine's.

From the light in the hallway, he could see her clothes were everywhere except her suitcase. Clean cotton lingerie in a rainbow of colors draped over the desk chair while an assortment of shorts and T-shirts took up residence on a bookcase. A long pink tank nightgown reclined on the bed as if she'd yanked it off the moment she opened her eyes.

The image didn't do a damn thing to settle his already hyperaware nerves.

Knowing the smart man's course of action should just

be to dump her on the bed and go, Vito couldn't help but think she'd sleep better without her shoes. Then again, he wasn't sure she'd thank him to undress any part of her.

"Vito?" Her voice startled him as his mind wandered off on a tangent about undressing her.

"Yeah?" He turned away from her feet to see her scooch herself up on the bed. Farther from him.

"What happened?" She blinked a few times as if to clear her vision.

Damn, he hoped she didn't clear it too fast because he was going to be giving her an eyeful if he stood up right now. How the hell could he carry her to bed without getting turned on? Willing himself into submission, he bought time by talking.

"You fell asleep on the tire swing so I brought you inside." And he hadn't even copped a feel while she was sleeping. Not really. "I figured you couldn't have been very comfortable out there."

She edged farther up the mattress to sit. "That's very nice of you, but I should probably go to bed now."

He recognized his cue to leave. Did she have to mention going to bed when he almost had himself back under control?

Down boy.

"You worked really hard today." He stalled. Reminded himself he was a thirty-five-year-old man and not a teenager. He could do this, damn it.

As long as he didn't think of her naked.

"I remember telling myself I'd only close my eyes for a few minutes and then—" She glanced at the bright green numbers on the clock display beside her bed. "I ended up sleeping for two hours."

Her voice took on that scratchy sleepy quality that made him think of staying in bed all day long.

An image that was no help to his current situation. Desperate for help, he glanced around the room, eyes lighting on a poster of his brother Nico that commemorated his first year in the NHL. Seeing Nico's ugly mug with his multibroken nose worked faster than a cold shower.

Vito sprang to his feet, welcoming a hasty retreat. "Then I guess I'd better leave you be. 'Night, Christine."

Hightailing out of her bedroom, Vito vowed to stay the hell out of there since he couldn't seem to stay in low gear around her. He wouldn't set foot in that bedroom again unless it was to fall into bed with the sexy garden goddess who'd taken up residence in his thoughts.

Although he'd be damn sure to yank down a few posters first.

CHRISTINE DEBATED leaping out her first-floor bedroom window the next morning so she wouldn't be forced to face Vito before she began her work outside.

But that hardly seemed the mature course of action. Besides, it might unveil her as a scaredy-cat or let Vito know she'd been avoiding him. And while she didn't mind being viewed as slightly unsophisticated, she couldn't stand the idea of appearing intimidated.

Unable to stall any longer, she wrenched open the door to her bedroom and marched out into the corridor to face the music. So she'd fallen asleep in the tire swing and had to be carried to bed by the sexy race-car driver who dominated her dreams. So what? It's not like she'd crawled between the sheets with him or anything.

Even if he had made her pulse race like the engine on one of those damn cars he drove.

She didn't need breakfast. She'd just slip out the kitchen door into the garage and get started on the watering. Pretend things were business as usual even though Vito's strong arms had been wrapped around her last night, all that delicious male muscle flexed solely for her benefit...

"Morning." His voice in the hallway behind her stopped her before she reached the dining room.

So much for slipping out without him noticing.

Turning, she saw him sauntering out of the bathroom as steam wafted into the hall. His towel was slung around his neck, and his bronze chest loomed—bare and inviting—within arm's reach. Could she help it if her gaze darted south to check out the rest of him? A pair of black cotton running shorts rode low on his hips, providing precious little barrier between her and...

Her mouth promptly went dry.

"You feel better today?" he prompted, stalking closer.

Closer? Christine backed up a step before realizing he only wanted to edge past her toward the kitchen. She sucked in a breath as he passed, determined to keep a few of her cranky boundaries around this man.

And although they managed to cross paths without touching, a hint of sporty aftershave sneaked past her defenses to tease her senses.

"I'm feeling just fine," she assured him. Despite the persistent weak-in-the-knees affliction that only struck when he was around. "Thank you for hauling me indoors last night."

She at least owed him that much, right? Somehow she'd neglected to thank him last night. Probably because she'd been too busy fighting off all those hormones.

He tossed his towel on a kitchen chair before pulling out the already steaming coffee pot and two mugs.

Two? She faltered on the perimeter of the wide-open, sunny kitchen.

"It was my pleasure." He met her gaze, his hazel eyes lingering on her until her temperature cranked up a few degrees and her skin tingled.

Oh, no, he didn't. He couldn't pull the Joe Suave act on her now and make her feel all awkward and turned on at the same time. She'd learned to deflect all the romantic BS men used when they wanted to pull a fast one on an unsuspecting female.

She might not have a superhero's fancy gold deflector bracelets, but she knew how to ignore loaded comments. Barreling through the kitchen toward the door, she chose to simply ignore the pleasure remark.

"Well, I'm off to work." She waved breezily, not bothering to make eye contact. "I'll take full responsibility for dragging my own tired butt back into the house tonight."

After the debacle with Rafe the bogus fiancé, she'd made a promise to herself not to give her heart away just because her inner romantic began to sigh dreamily. And God knows, Vito Cesare could wrest a dreamy sigh from the most hardened of hearts.

She almost tasted freedom. The kitchen door was already cracked, her fast-moving feet barely pausing on the mat as she made her getaway.

Then Vito's hand covered hers, his big, male body moving even closer than it had in the hallway as he inserted himself between her and her escape.

"Hold up a minute. We need to talk." He held himself there, so close she could feel his breath on her cheek.

"We do?" She didn't particularly want to converse with a man so good-looking he ought to have the word *Heartbreaker* stamped across his world-class pecs. Possibly on his very cute butt, as well.

A girl could use all the help she could get when faced with this kind of temptation.

"I spoke with my uncle again last night." He inched

back a step, giving her enough space to breathe again. Think.

Slowly, information began to process in her head again, proving she wasn't controlled by her hormones. At least not all the time.

"You did?" She moved back toward the kitchen counter where he nudged a cup of coffee toward her.

Vito had been trying to have a long discussion with his uncle ever since he'd arrived in the States, but apparently Giuseppe was very good at wriggling his way out of any extended conversations. The only thing Vito had managed to clear up the day after he'd arrived back home was that Giuseppe had definitely hired Christine and that he was sorry for any inconvenience it caused, but he wanted it to be his gift to Giselle.

Fine.

But as soon as that much had been settled, Giuseppe had come up with one excuse after another not to chat with Vito, including—most recently—a trip to the Florida Keys. Any time Vito began a conversation about his uncle's matchmaking problem, Giuseppe was off the phone before he could blink.

"I didn't get to talk to him for long because he was getting ready to leave on a snorkeling trip." Vito rolled his eyes. "He did confirm he wanted a hummingbird garden in one corner of the lawn because apparently hummingbirds are Giselle's favorite. But when I tried to explain the problems he'd created by having us both staying in the house and asked him if he was up to his old tricks, he pretended to have no idea what I meant.''

Christine bristled even though her first sip of Vito's coffee was like the nectar of the gods. Fantastic.

''Maybe he hired me for my great portfolio after all.'' Vito's uncle had seemed really impressed with her pictures of other jobs she'd completed in California.

''He wouldn't have hired you if your work wasn't fantastic.'' He glanced out the kitchen window overlooking the yard. ''I'll admit I was worried when I first came home and saw the whole place torn up, but I'm beginning to see what you're going for now and I think it's going to look great.''

''Better than great.'' She'd never been an arrogant woman, but she knew without a doubt the Cesare property would be spectacular. Warm and inviting with gardens that beckoned passersby, the yard would be a natural haven in the midst of urban sprawl. ''You'll never want to go back to Italy once you see your house in its new finery. I was thinking maybe I'd leave my business card with Mary Jo once I finish up so if anyone asks her who did your yard, she can spread the word.''

She'd been thinking about that, hoping it didn't seem too intrusive. But if she wanted her business to flourish she needed to stabilize the roots. As a gardener, she knew this, but she'd never been one to tout her own accomplishments.

Vito was frowning, however.

"I don't have to mention it to Mrs. K. if you don't want me to."

"It's not that." He replaced his mug on the countertop, his bare shoulders rippling with lean muscle from even that small movement. "I just thought you'd be here for a few more weeks. You're not going to be finished anytime soon, are you?"

She shrugged as she sipped coffee that was as warm and tasty as she knew he would be. She'd really been much better off not knowing what he looked like without his shirt.

Yum.

"Less than a month. I want everything to be finished by the time out-of-town company starts rolling in."

He rolled his eyes, a grin playing about his lips. "You don't understand Italian weddings. Out-of-town company will probably start arriving next week. My whole extended family will want to have a hand in helping Giselle get ready for the big day."

"You're kidding." She loved her family, but the Chandlers had always given one another a lot of room. She couldn't picture having family around her for weeks before her big day. She'd probably elope before she let anyone make that big a fuss over her.

"Nope. They'll be here before we know it, which means we only have so much time to enjoy…the quiet." He nodded toward her empty coffee cup. "Can you sit for a few minutes while I cook you breakfast? Although

I have to confess you've already sampled the one thing I make well in the kitchen.''

Actually, she'd stake her paycheck that the two of them could make something very well right here. Against the kitchen counter. Or maybe sprawled across the table.

But she couldn't let herself think about that when she had a long day of work ahead of her. Besides, she didn't allow herself to lust after men like Vito Cesare. Too dangerous. Too temporary.

Because, no matter how much she told herself that she could scratch the occasional itch with a man as long as she didn't allow herself to think ridiculous, romantic thoughts, Vito posed too much of a threat on every level.

What woman wouldn't start thinking loopy, mushy thoughts if she stared into those dark hazel eyes long enough?

''Thanks, but I need to pass on breakfast today if I want to get a jump on things before it heats up any more.'' She moved toward the door before she remembered the whole reason Vito needed to talk to her this morning. ''So what else did your uncle have to say?''

''Besides denying that he played matchmaker this time? He also asked me to go over your work when you're finished and then he'll make sure you receive your check right away. In fact, he told me that you weren't just a landscaper, you're an artist.'' He followed her across the kitchen where she'd paused. Frozen.

Too close to his half-naked bod.

"Really?" She swallowed, flattered by the compliment but too flustered by Vito's bronze chest sprinkled with silky dark hair to fully enjoy the words.

"Yeah." Vito reached out to touch her, his knuckles grazing the back of her hair. "But if you wanted to get outside before things heated up today, I think you're already too late."

5

VITO HAD SPOTTED the reciprocal attraction in Christine's eyes, so he thought this morning was as good a time as any to step up the pace on his summer seduction.

But he realized as soon as he touched her that he'd miscalculated. Overstepped those damn boundaries of hers too soon. A flash of something akin to panic blazed in her gaze for a split second, warning him off course before he crashed and burned.

Time to nail the brakes.

"Excuse me?" Christine glared daggers at him, all hints of fear well concealed under convincing-as-hell anger.

Jamming his wayward hand into the pocket of his shorts, he nodded toward the kitchen window and the view of the relentless sunshine filling the backyard. "I just said you're not going to beat the heat today. Thermometer says it's already eighty-four."

He hid a smile while she frowned at him. He couldn't remember the last time he'd had to work this hard for a woman, and damned if he wasn't enjoying himself even as she scowled. How sick was that?

"Don't mess with me, Cesare." She pointed a finger at him, her gaze narrowed. "I've got my eye on you."

He did his best to look innocent while he opened the door for her. "I'm flattered. Let me know if you need help with anything."

Pushing past him amid a great deal of harrumphing, Christine and her heavy work boots stomped outside. Vito lingered in the doorway for a moment to watch her go, trying to put his finger on what exactly he found so attractive about her.

It was more than just the thrill of the chase, although he had to admit he enjoyed pursuing a woman who had no interest in his famous career or equally famous fortune. He was in second place for the most lifetime winnings on his circuit and with another good year behind the wheel he had a strong chance of taking the first place spot.

Not that he was in it for the money, but plenty of women had flirted with him for that reason alone. He liked that Christine had simpler values and a fierce independent streak. His father had raised him to be self-sufficient long before Vito made truckloads of money as a driver, and he'd always admired that same quality in other people.

As he watched Christine stare at the yard with a critical eye, her dark head turning this way and that, he realized her perfectionist streak held an appeal of its own. Her hard work in the gardens day after day revealed a woman with high standards who didn't mind working hard—or getting her hands dirty—to achieve them. Something about that characteristic of hers called to him on the most elemental level. A woman like that would make a strong partner. An awesome wife.

Had he just thought *wife?*

Ducking back into the cool air-conditioning of the house, Vito decided the Florida sun must be scrambling his brains. He wanted Christine Chandler because she was sexy as hell and because watching her day after day seriously compromised his ability to do anything except fantasize about her.

He'd continue with his plan to woo her, but he'd have to maintain an easy pace if he didn't want to scare her off. Maybe the time had come to make a trip out to the outdoor shower and pay her a surprise visit.

Smiling at his plan, Vito couldn't wait for night to arrive.

CHRISTINE made damn sure she quit work early that night. Hauling her tools back to the workshop, she double-checked her watch.

Not that ten o'clock was early by a normal person's standards, but it meant she wouldn't be so exhausted she'd fall asleep in the yard. She'd gotten a case of delicious shivers every time she envisioned Vito carrying her to bed last night. Which made no sense given that she was so determined to keep her distance from him and his slick charm honed to perfection at too many glitzy European parties.

Or so she imagined as she stood the rake against the wall of the shed and peeled off her work gloves.

She actually had no idea what Vito's life might be like abroad, but she'd concocted an image in her mind of weekends on the Riviera and cruises on the Mediterranean. All of which included topless beaches and sophisticated women draped all over him.

She was *so* not into that. Slipping out of her work boots, she padded to the back of the shed in her socks. Give her a plot of land and some flowers and she could be happy. Okay, toss in a few friends and loved ones who didn't talk out of both sides of their faces and then she'd be even happier. She liked people who were honest. Real.

Not people who built their whole world on glamour and pretense.

Trouble was, she couldn't decide if the real Vito preferred his Gucci shoes or his flip-flops. His Ferrari that he'd taken out of storage, or his pickup truck bearing a logo for his brother's construction firm. From what she could see, he actually spent more time on his computer than anything. He left the house occasionally to do some errands, but for the most part, he worked on a sleek laptop for hours on end.

Christine tucked into the back corner of the work space where an abandoned desk blocked the rear exit of the building. The doorway led to the outdoor shower where she'd begun to wash every night since Vito had arrived home. It only made sense to clean up before she went inside anyhow, and it saved her the awkward passing of one another in the hallway. She kept a bag with a few clothes out here along with soap and shampoo.

And although she didn't anticipate anyone walking into the small building late at night, she still took the extra precaution of changing in the enclosed shower stall. Just in case.

She wouldn't want some unsuspecting neighbor to drop by while she was dropping her drawers, only to be the subject of one of Mary Jo Kowolski's stories for years to come.

Dragging a clean T-shirt and cotton shorts into the stall, she tossed them over the six-foot-high wooden walls along with the dirty outfit. Taking time to stare up at the moon and stars, she flicked on the water and reveled in the mix of warm night air and slight steam from the shower.

Divine. If she could ever afford her own home with property, she would install one of these babies herself. Her feet rested on smooth, sloped stones while the water ran down into a grate off to one side. When the nights were superhumid, she took a cold shower, but she was so filthy tonight she craved the sterilizing effects of hot water.

Humming to herself, she scrubbed and soaped until the shower began to cool. Rinsing the last of the bubbles from her hair, she reluctantly finished her bedtime ritual. She reached for her towel and realized it wasn't there just as a voice came from the other side of the shower wall.

"Did you lose this?" Vito's hand appeared over the enclosure wall, holding her towel between his fingers.

Awareness fired through her faster than embarrassment. Hearing his voice while she stood naked and dripping...

"I need that." She started to reach for the towel and then wondered if he would see her if she got too close to the wall. Didn't he stand over six feet himself?

"Can you...um...just hang it on the wall, perhaps?" She shivered. Wrapped her arms around herself.

And it wasn't anywhere near cold outside.

"I don't mind bringing it in there to you if that would help." He waited. Held the damn towel just above the wall.

"I think you know that wouldn't be the least bit helpful." She wrung out her short hair and tried not to let him fluster her. Flirting was a way of life for men like him. She just couldn't let him see that he affected her a teeny, tiny bit. "Do I look like some racing groupie dying to get naked with you? Get over yourself, Cesare, and give me the damn towel."

"Have it your way. Just trying to be helpful." The length of fluffy blue terry cloth came sailing over the wall of the stall. "Out of curiosity, what would you have done if I hadn't come along to rescue your towel?"

Wrapping the linen around herself in record time even though she knew he couldn't possibly see her through the wooden latticework and the interior privacy wall, Christine glowered at him right through the barrier. "I certainly wouldn't have run around your yard naked, if that's what you're thinking."

"Of course that's what I'm thinking. It's a guy thing to continually conjure up scenarios where women get naked."

She tugged a clean T-shirt over her head. "Fine. Conjure away then. Just please don't include me in the myriad of ever-changing male fantasies, okay? I'm working too hard for you to diminish my contribution with idle flirtation."

For a long moment, the only response from the other side of the wall was the call of a night bird.

She felt a bit self-conscious as she slid into her shorts, every rustle of fabric sounding loud to her own ears. Could he envision her every move from the soft noises she made?

Eager simply to put the whole incident behind them, she shoved open the door to the shed and tossed her towel and her dirty clothes into a laundry bag before zipping her small bag for the night. Combing her fingers through her short hair, she walked through the workshop and shut off the lights before exiting onto the lawn.

Vito stood a few feet from the shower stall in the darkness, a tiny sliver of a moon doing little to light the yard or his expression. He wore a dark collared shirt with a pair of slouchy shorts, his flip-flops slapping the ground as he stepped closer.

"Do you really think me flirting with you diminishes you in any way in my eyes?" The teasing tone had vanished from his voice.

Sighing, she searched for a way to put them back on neutral ground. "Not necessarily. I guess I'm just a little defensive about any potential hanky-panky between us after what you told me about your uncle hiring me as a potential hookup for you."

"I never said that's what Uncle Giuseppe was trying to do, damn it. He's just an old guy with a big heart. And he'd sure as hell never endorse something so sordid sounding as a hookup."

"You're right. That was my spin on it, and I realize you never put it that way. Sorry." She needed to get to the house. Away from Vito and all talk of hooking up. "I just meant that I'm a little sensitive about any dynamic that could be construed as flirtation between us because I don't want your uncle to be right about this. About us."

And since that was more than her quota for emotional honesty tonight, she turned on her heel in the soft ground she'd prepped for sodding today and headed back to the house.

For all of two steps.

"Wait a minute." His hand slid around her elbow, warm fingers settling along her skin. "Don't tell me you're going to let Giuseppe's ridiculous romantic streak affect you one way or the other. If you don't want me to make stupid jokes about picturing women naked, I can completely respect that. But if you had any inclination to—"

"Get undressed with *you?*" It seemed silly to avoid the words when they both had to be thinking the same thing. Too bad she shared Giuseppe's ridiculous romanticism while Vito seemed more inclined to take "naked" whenever and wherever he could find it.

Vito shrugged, relinquishing her arm. "Just don't let my crazy family influence you either way."

She couldn't deny her skin felt lonelier without his touch. Hugging herself in the dark, humid night air, she scrubbed her hands along her arms as if to erase the memory of that gentle caress. A soft breeze rustled the palm branches above them.

"I don't know, Vito." She didn't want to think about him or her or being stripped down anymore. Not when she had an important job to finish. A business to build.

She knew better than to mess up her life's dream by screwing around, didn't she? Of course she did.

"Can you talk to me for a minute?" Vito pulled her around the new paver stones she'd installed earlier in the day and led her to the small stretch of existing patio she'd salvaged. He held out a chair for her, the same chair she'd sat in the first day he'd arrived and turned her world on its ear. "Sit with me, Christine."

Too tired to protest, she thought it might be easier in this instance to simply agree. Lowering herself into the seat, she watched him move around the glass-topped table to pull the other chair closer.

Right beside her.

Some of her exhaustion leaked away, replaced by nerves. Awareness.

Words tumbled out of her mouth to fill the heated air between them. "You're going to love the new patio once it's surrounded by more greenery. I'm going to plant so much night-blooming jasmine back here it will be like walking into a hothouse every night when you step out on the deck."

"I'm sorry." He propped an elbow on the table as he leaned closer. "I want to hear more about the landscaping plans, Christine, but first let me just say I'm sorry for interrupting your shower."

"It's not a big deal." Geesh, she shouldn't have acted like such a harassment-suit-happy whiner about the whole thing. He hadn't offended her so much as he tempted her, but she wasn't sure how to tell him that now without the conversation taking a turn she definitely wasn't prepared for.

"I admit I was trying to rile you a little bit, just to see what would happen." He raked a hand through his dark hair, the tousled strands conspiring with the neatly shaved hair at his chin to make him look even more dangerous. Sexy. "I thought I sensed some chemistry between us and I guess I've been looking for a way to turn up the heat without coming on to you and making you mad. But I guess I did that anyway."

"I'm not mad." She just wanted the hell out of this conversation. The sooner the better. She'd had good luck avoiding Vito and the chemistry in question for the last two weeks, and now here he was, dragging it all out into the open.

The whole reason she'd ended up falling in love via the Internet was because she stank at conversations where you needed to examine feelings and share thoughts face-to-face. At least in e-mails you could maintain a hint of distance and take your time responding. She appreciated the chance to weigh her options and tweak her answers before hitting the send button.

Right now, face-to-face with Vito, she had the feeling no matter what she said—fact or fiction—she'd be kicking herself in the morning.

VITO HAD all of nature playing on his side. Moonlight, warm breezes and other than the occasional call of a night bird, the neighborhood remained quiet. Private.

Plus the fact that he'd caught Christine in the shower earlier, and the whole equation should add up to the two of them exchanging mind-numbing kisses and falling into his bed. Instead he found himself in sticky terrain with a woman who looked as though she would bolt if he didn't tie her down.

An idea that wasn't totally lacking in merit.

"If you're not mad at me..." he forged ahead, unable to forgo his plans for seduction even when they were exploding in his face. The thought of her in that shower every night had been making him crazy. "...then hear me out. I have a proposition to make."

Eyes widening, Christine edged to the far side of her chair. Possibly to look at him without turning her head since they were seated so close together at the patio table. But Vito knew damn well she was inserting space between them.

"You'd prefer honeysuckle over the Virginia creeper wouldn't you?" she supplied, her gaze flicking over a new vine she'd planted along the back of the house.

Sliding his hand over hers where it rested on the arm of her chair, his touch succeeded in securing her attention far better than his words had done.

"I guarantee my idea doesn't have a damn thing to do with flowers." He absorbed the smooth feel of the skin she protected every day with gloves despite the heat. The rapid beat of her heart pulsed through her veins as he stroked his thumb over the back of her hand.

He wished he could tell himself that fluttering of her heart came from attraction, but his gut told him it had more to do with anxiety. He made her nervous for some reason. So much so that she was starting to make *him* nervous, for crying out loud.

Propositioning a woman had never been so bloody difficult.

"Remember when you told me that men weren't in your five-year plan?" He'd been thinking about those words for two weeks, assuring himself he hadn't misunderstood.

"I remember," she replied carefully, staring down at their joined hands as if trying to catalog some never-seen-before plant species. "Maybe I should have mentioned that showering in the vicinity of men was also not on my agenda."

Ah, hell. There was no hope to bring this up subtly.

Vito took a deep breath and spoke his peace.

"After you confided that, it occurred to me that we would be ideal candidates for a summer fling."

He recognized that his delivery lacked romance and passion and all that hearts-and-flowers stuff women liked. He hadn't needed to employ charm for so long he wondered if he still possessed a supply.

"A fling?" Her jaw dropped. She slid her hand out from under his then wrapped her arms around herself in the warm night air. Shadows drifted over her face as clouds covered the moon, making her reaction all the more difficult to gauge.

"Yes. From what you said about not wanting a relationship, I thought a no-strings-attached affair might have a certain appeal." He hoped. "That is, if I haven't misread you. I was under the impression the attraction between us might be mutual."

"I'm never even around you since I'm outdoors and you're inside on the computer all the time." She shook her head, her dark hair bobbing around her face with the effort. "I've avoided you at all costs for two weeks and counting." She frowned as she glared at him. "Just how in the blazes would you decide I must be attracted to you? Is this some racer-ego thing at work where you must have every woman within a mile radius of you?"

"I promise this has nothing to do with ego and everything to do with libido." It also had something to do with *her*, since she fired him up in a way no woman other woman had. "And I guessed maybe you were attracted because you were avoiding me at all costs for two weeks and counting."

She smacked the tabletop with her hand. "And from that you assume I must want you?" Her voice rose with the sentiment before her gaze narrowed. "How do you know you don't just have bad breath?"

"Okay, so maybe there's a little ego involved in this part. Plus I have a really great dentist." He leaned back in his chair to give her time to think. To get out of her face for a minute and maybe take some of the pressure off. He'd never seen anyone fight physical attraction with such dogged determination.

Staring up at the stars, he mentally connected the dots to make the Big Dipper. Waiting.

"I might be a little bit attracted." Her soft-spoken honesty came when he'd least expected it, her words as straightforward and honest as her work ethic. Simple. Strong.

Forgetting all about the night sky, Vito leaned closer. His first instinct was to shout "aha!" but he thought that wouldn't go over well. Unlike his brothers, he didn't need to speak his every thought.

Most of the time, anyway.

"We don't have to do anything about it, obviously." But he really, really wanted to. "I just thought it could be fun to see what happens if we act on it."

Staring out over the yard in the shifting moonlight, Christine finally dragged her gaze back to his. "But I don't know about the...fling. I'll admit the idea sounds intriguing."

Her eyes flitted away again, bouncing down to the table, up to the house, anywhere but toward him.

And just like that, his engine started heating up into the red zone. Knowing that she was thinking about him, and that thinking about him rattled her... Vito couldn't imagine what kind of reaction he'd get if he kissed her, touched her, undressed every inch of her.

"It's intriguing me, too," he admitted, hoping honesty would make up for what his proposal had lacked in finesse. "I've been thinking about you a lot lately."

She glanced back at him finally, her fingers drumming a high-speed tune on the arm of her patio chair. "But I need to think over your suggestion. Just because I'm curious doesn't give me the right to jump into bed with someone. I'd like to take a few days to decide."

Days? He'd been hoping she'd say minutes. Or maybe hours. He could have waited a few hours and then hauled her back to his bed to explore every sweet inch of her.

"Fair enough," he lied, knowing it was the right thing to say even if he'd suffer mightily while she made up her mind. "But can I ask you to take one more thing into consideration before you make up your mind?"

His blood slogged through his veins with heavy, hot force but he held himself perfectly still until she nodded.

And then, slanting his lips over hers, he employed a more eloquent means of persuasion.

6

VITO'S KISS acted on Christine's decision-making powers with all the potency of Miracle-Gro.

She had wanted to be so smart about this, so reasonable, yet the warm heat of his mouth on hers made it nearly impossible for her to refuse him. Urged her to say yes, right then and there.

Lifting her hands to his shoulders, she told herself she should insert some space between them. Yet her fingers failed to push him away. They tracked their way down his chest, savoring the broad, masculine feel of him without her permission.

Shifting in her seat, she found herself closer to him. If not for the arm of her chair she might have been in his lap. His tongue stroked over hers with slow thoroughness, forcing her to remember she couldn't deny herself male companionship for years on end while she got her business off the ground. She wasn't a slave to her work.

She was a woman with very real physical desires. Needs. And this whole idea of a fling was making more and more sense to her passion-clouded brain. Especially when Vito's hand landed on her bare knee.

Christine broke away from him before she lost all control.

"I will keep that point in mind while I think things over," she blurted, desperate for space before she combusted right in front of him.

Rising on shaky legs, she moved away from the table. "Your last thought on the subject was particularly convincing."

He shot to his feet. "I didn't mean to...spend so much time making the argument." The half smile he gave her stole away her very last defense. "That kiss sort of took on a life of its own."

She backed away across the patio toward the French doors leading into the house. "No need to stand on my account." She waved him away while she made her escape. "I'm just going to head to bed anyway."

If he'd been the player she'd once accused him of being, he would have asked to join her. Or worse, used another kiss on her to change her mind. God knows she'd proven herself susceptible.

But he remained right where she left him by the patio table, his hands jammed into his pockets.

"'Night, Christine."

This time he didn't have to wish her pleasant dreams. They both knew exactly what she'd be thinking about tonight.

DAYS passed.

Christine bent over the roots of an uncooperative fig

tree nearly a week later and told herself she had to give Vito an answer one way or another soon. She'd told him she'd get back to him in a few days' time, but ever since he'd kissed her she'd been plagued with indecision.

Should she? Shouldn't she?

The temptation persisted even while her logical mind made all sorts of rational arguments. Really smart rational arguments. Like, why should she ever subject herself to romantic involvement again after the valuable lesson she'd learned last time? Those cartoon hearts in her eyes sure had clouded her judgment with Rafe.

Digging a circle around the base of the transplanted tree, she was attempting to stabilize the unsteady fig when she heard the door to the house slam.

Vito.

Her heart picked up a ridiculous rhythm while she kept her eyes focused on the goal. Fix the damn tree. Figure out what to do about Vito later.

"I hear it's going to be a scorcher today." His voice rumbled along her senses as he paused at the edge of the driveway. Dressed in a wheat-colored linen jacket and dark slacks, he looked too sleek for her, much like the curvy Ferrari in the driveway behind him. Unfortunately, her rapid-fire pulse thought he looked just fine.

"No news there." She stood her shovel on the ground and leaned on the handle. "It's been hot for days."

The words barely left her lips before she realized they

sounded like a come-on. Or did they just sound that way to her because she had sex on the brain lately?

"Doesn't look like there's an end in sight for the heat wave, does there?" His hazel eyes bored into her for a long moment, making her all too aware of the temperature. Inside and out.

Her throat dried up like a neglected houseplant. Apparently, she wasn't the only one suffering from sex on the brain.

Before she could snap out of it, Vito was sliding into the driver's seat of his low-slung sports car.

"You're killing me, Christine." His words mingled with the rumble of the engine as he turned the key, and then drove out of sight.

Damn.

He thought *she* was killing *him?* Didn't he know this decision was eating her up inside, too? Tormenting her all night with sexy dreams when she should be sleeping like a log?

Guilt pinched her as she turned back to the matter of the fig tree. It wasn't fair to keep Vito wondering when she'd said she'd get back to him in a few days. She could only avoid him—and the inevitable attraction she felt every time she so much as glanced his way—for so long.

Her legs suddenly as shaky as the unsteady fruit tree, Christine wished it could be as easy to solve her problem as it was to fix the sapling. All the fig needed was some more dirt. Then, with a little water and a bit of sunshine, the tree would put down roots to keep it healthy for years to come.

But what would stop her legs from shaking? Burying herself in work clearly wasn't helping. If anything, being so distracted by Vito and the surges of desire he inspired probably hurt her job performance. The poor fig tree might have been standing tall this morning if she hadn't been sneaking covert glances at Vito stripping off his shirt while he fixed the broken garage door opener yesterday.

Maybe she needed to stop worrying so much about getting caught up in romantic fairy tales that would only disillusion her and start taking a more practical approach to men. What if she simply fed her own needs the way she nurtured her plants? Quit denying herself basic human sustenance.

Like sex.

It was sort of a physiological need, wasn't it? She seemed to recall some hierarchy of needs she'd learned in school that placed sex right after food and shelter.

No wonder her legs were shaking. She was malnourished.

She walked a circle around the tree to tamp down the dirt against the slender trunk. New energy seemed to spark in her veins. Anticipation?

Definitely.

It had taken her almost all week, but she'd finally figured out how to indulge herself just this once without getting ensnared in her usual overinflated expectations of relationships. She would have a fling with Vito, damn it. And she wouldn't do it because she had cartoon hearts in her eyes.

She would do it as an act of self-nurturing. To fulfill a basic need. And to keep herself from losing her mind while she toiled away at the most challenging job of her career.

It was all perfectly practical.

HOW MANY DAYS was it going to take her to put him out of his damn misery?

Thinking of the heat wave sweltering between him and Christine, Vito grumbled to himself late that afternoon while he reviewed the menu for Giselle's wedding at Club Paradise in South Beach.

Because his sister still owned a share of the exotic resort, she wanted her reception at the house to be catered by the hotel's restaurant. And since she'd created the menu during her time as chef at Club Paradise, Vito thought it shouldn't be too damn hard for her to choose what she wanted.

That didn't stop her from asking him to go over everything anyway since he was standing in as father of the bride for her. It was a role he normally wouldn't mind, but somehow today it made him feel ancient when all his younger siblings were marrying off so quickly.

Struggling to banish images of Christine's trim ankles encased in work boots from his mind, he tried to focus on the list of a thousand and one appetizers in front of him so he could scratch another item off his list before the wedding. Still, the view of the ocean beckoned from his outdoor table in the hotel's café-style restaurant, the deep blue calling to mind Christine's eyes.

Club Paradise might be a steamy singles resort with a reputation for provocative theme rooms, but the overt, sex-drenched atmosphere didn't light his fire the way Christine could with her lean, toned muscles and her long, tanned legs. He'd never again be able to see a pair of women's work boots without getting seriously turned on.

"How's it going?" Lainie Reynolds, the resort's CEO, who also happened to be engaged to his brother Nico, breezed into view. Her sleek blond hair swung neatly around her shoulders, her simple red coatdress lacking any sign of creases.

How his sports-crazy, outspoken brother had ended up with someone so damn smart and together, Vito had no clue.

"Honestly, I don't know goat cheese from Gouda. I just want to write the damn check and be done with my part of the wedding preparations." He loved his sister and all, but he had more things to do today besides labor over the food selections. Besides, he thought spaghetti sounded better than anything on the menu.

Lainie plucked the paper out of his hand. "Why don't I give it a once-over for you? I can make sure Giselle didn't miss anything while I see if there are any good menu ideas I should snitch when Nico and I tie the knot next spring."

"Is my brother still trying to talk you into getting married in Kentucky?" Apparently Lainie hailed from the remote Appalachian area of the Bluegrass State, a surprise to all her South Beach friends who'd assumed the former attorney and business dynamo had been born someplace more Ivy League.

"He's had his heart set on it ever since we took the trip up there a few weeks ago." She flicked her hair over one shoulder, the sunlight catching the fat diamond ring Nico had placed on one of her perfectly manicured fingers. "I think I'm going to give it the thumbs-up as long as he promises not to wear buckskins. Did I mention he's really into the whole mountain-man thing?"

"I'll definitely be there. And I want you to know I'm really happy for you both." As he withdrew his check-book from the pocket of his linen jacket, Vito had to hand it to his brother for landing the woman of his dreams. Everyone in his family would be married off within a year except for him and Marco.

Not that Vito minded. He'd left Miami to put his days of domestic duties and child-raising responsibilities behind him and hadn't looked back since. Although he had to admit, looking at how happy Lainie and Nico were together made him wonder if there might be more to wedded bliss than he realized.

"Thanks, Vito." Lainie bent to kiss his cheek. "And it's only fair that I warn you, since we're almost family now—Nico and Renzo agree you're overdue to find a bride. Apparently something about being in love is turning them both into muscle-bound cupids. I'd be on the lookout for potential matchmaking efforts."

Vito's pen stalled as he wrote out a check to the resort. Then, adding a few more zeros to the sum, he scrawled his name and passed it to his future sister-in-law.

"You're a good woman, Lainie. I appreciate the warning, but there's not much I can do to duck the determined efforts of the whole clan. I've even got a sixty-year-old widowed uncle on my case. I'm just going to resign myself to catching the blasted garter at Giselle's wedding and pray whoever catches the bouquet at least has all her teeth."

Briefly, he wondered if Christine could ever be persuaded to attend the wedding. He tried to imagine her without her work boots, her slender feet in delicate high heels. Maybe she could dance with him instead of some jet-set sophisticate friend of his sister's.

Then again, if he showed up at his sister's wedding with a date in front of his entire extended family, he might as well propose to her then and there because his relatives would probably never let her escape.

Business concluded, Vito left Lainie to her job while he wandered back inside the hotel. His phone rang and he answered it while he studied the latest erotic statuary added to the collection in the lobby. He never had any problem with straightforward classical pieces, but this modern stuff that was all body parts...forget it.

Squinting, he thought he'd deciphered a woman's fingers spreading her own thighs by the time he said hello.

"I've got a race for you in Germany the second week of September." The clipped British accent of his publicist, Oswald Martin, crackled through the cell phone.

"Hey, Ozzie. Nice to talk to you, too." For a publicist, the man sure didn't waste time with niceties for his client. Vito tore his gaze away from the smooth marble rendering of a woman's splayed thighs. He didn't need any more sensual incentives while he waited for Christine to make up her mind about his proposition. "I've got a commitment here on the first, remember?"

"As long as you leave the States the next day, you should be well-rested in time for the race. Shall I make the arrangements?"

Oddly, Vito's first thought was for Christine. But why should it matter to her when he left? She hadn't even given him any indication she would accept his offer of a fling, let alone any reason to linger in Miami.

He'd made damn sure he had no ties in his life, nothing to prevent him from pursuing his own dreams after putting them aside while his youngest brother and his sister grew up. There was still nothing to keep him here.

Although for some reason, maybe talking to Lainie about her wedding plans, that freedom he'd always valued didn't give him the usual thrill today.

"Yeah. Sign me on. Let me know when you get things finalized." Vito finished up his call and walked away from the display case full of erotic statues.

A race would do him good. He needed the adrenaline rush that came with two-hundred-mile-an-hour speeds to clear his head. After days of heady sexual fantasies and wondering whether Christine Chandler wanted to sleep with him or not, he craved the mental clarity that routinely settled over him as he achieved top performance on the raceway.

He'd almost reached the lobby doors when his phone rang again.

"Yeah?" He didn't bother with niceties since the only people who had the cell phone number were his closest friends and family.

Although he'd also given it to one other person...

"Vito?" Christine's throaty voice vibrated through the earpiece, stopping him cold in his tracks.

"Is everything okay at the house?" He didn't like the idea of her working alone, doing hard physical labor, in the ungodly Florida heat. What if something had happened to her?

"Everything's fine. More than fine. I just wanted to let you know that I'd like to take you up on your offer."

CHRISTINE hadn't been sure if the strangled sounds Vito made in response to her decision were good or bad. Had he changed his mind about wanting a fling?

His only intelligible words had been, "I'm on my way."

Since she had no idea where he was at the time, she couldn't begin to guess when she might see him. Hanging up the phone, she'd decided to go back to work to take her mind off her the impending encounter with Vito. Now, testing the new sprinkler system she'd installed that afternoon, Christine watched as the multiple spigots popped up around the lawn according to her commands on the digital controls mounted in the garage.

She'd ended her day early for a change. After weeks of hard work, she could see the end of the project in sight. The next two weeks before the wedding would be less physically intense as she coaxed the new sod to take root and carefully fertilized all the new flower beds to bloom. There were still smaller projects that needed tending, such as the hunt for antique planters and a birdbath to complement the gardens, but they required less energy.

Leaving her to expend her energy elsewhere. Such as Vito's bed, if he was still willing.

The idea gave her shivers in spite of the late-day heat. Christine walked around the property, making a game of ducking the sprinklers as she inspected her work. She'd already showered and changed into a simple knit sundress, so she refused to give into the urge to fiddle with the plants anymore.

Still, she was about to straighten a drooping wax

myrtle branch when she heard the low growl of Vito's sports car in the driveway. Nerves raining over her body faster than the drops from the sprinkler, she let the branch fall where it may.

Straightening, she peered toward the car and the tall, sleek man unfolding himself from the driver's seat. His gaze sought her out right away. Locked on her as he strode closer.

Her heart picked up speed and she told herself it was simply because she'd never had a fling before and not because Vito Cesare inspired heady romantic fantasies. Her decision to have an affair with him had nothing to do with romance and everything to do with practicality. She had needs. She couldn't ignore them forever.

And it just so happened Vito wanted to fulfill those needs. End of story.

The fact that the man gave new meaning to the word *sexy* was just a bonus.

Fanning the fabric of her sundress in an effort to dry the drops from the sprinkler, she tried not to notice as he closed the space between them to mere inches.

"Back so soon?" Her words didn't sound quite as steady as she would have liked. But there was no denying the man made her nervous. Excited.

"No point having a Ferrari if I can't get where I want to go in a hurry." He took a step closer, which would have put him right on top of her if she hadn't taken a step back. "Would you care to repeat what you told me on the phone now that I'm in a position to fully appreciate it?"

More heat rolled off him than off the blistering tarmac. The linen jacket he'd been wearing when he left the house that morning was gone, leaving him in a white silk T-shirt and black trousers.

She found herself very ready to touch him. To see if he felt as good as she remembered.

"I said I was ready to take you up on your offer." Licking her lips, she decided if he didn't kiss her soon, she'd take the initiative herself. Her attack of nerves seemed to be fading as desire flowed through her veins instead.

"It's been a hell of a long time since we talked over any offers, Christine. Days and days and too many hours to count. You think maybe you could refresh my memory on what you're saying 'yes' to, so that there can't be any mistake?" Dark frustration lurked behind his words, but it didn't take away from the hunger in his eyes.

The idea of him waiting for her, wanting her, shoved aside the last vestiges of her worries. And heaven knew, she could appreciate a man who didn't want to play games, who wanted things spelled out clearly.

Yes, this bargain of theirs would work out very, very well.

She peered up at him in the last rays of the setting sun. "I'm referring to your offer for traded sensual pleasures within a finite time frame. You had a name for it, I believe?" Tapping her chin thoughtfully with one finger, she smiled. "Oh yes, I remember. A fling. I'm agreeing to all that entails, starting today."

"Do you have any idea how a fling is conducted?" He looked suspicious. Doubtful.

"I think I'm offended by the question. Do I behave like a woman who has a lot of experience with this sort of thing?" Exasperated with the process, she sighed. "I had rather hoped to have arrived at the kissing portion of this business by now."

He nodded. Slowly. "That sounds like a damn good place to start."

His hands framed her face, tilting her chin until he'd achieved just the right angle before his mouth met hers. Soft. Warm. Slick.

He tasted her with dizzying thoroughness, his lips molding to hers as their bodies drifted closer. Closer. The heat of the blazing Florida day just before sunset was nothing compared to the heat of Vito's body. Her skin seemed to sizzle at the slightest contact.

Twining her arms around his neck, she plastered herself to him as he backed them deeper into the dim recesses of the garage, away from prying neighborhood eyes. No longer plagued with concerns about maintaining professional distance or personal boundaries, Christine was more than ready to take this to the next level. They'd made a deal after all.

A fling was a harmless affair with a limited time

frame and an assured outcome. They both went their separate ways afterward.

No one got hurt and her job wouldn't be compromised. It was perfect. Delicious. And just exactly what she needed in her life right now as a sweet reward for her hard work to make it on her own.

"Where?" Vito muttered against her mouth, breaking the kiss only for a moment in the corner of the garage.

She moved his hand from its innocent resting place on her shoulder and nudged it south to the aching curve of her...ahh. Breast.

He groaned in time with her sigh, his fingers automatically swirling a caress along the neck of her sundress.

"I meant where do you want to take this?" Vito pulled back long enough to look at her as his fingers shifted beneath the cotton fabric. "I promise I'll know where to touch you if you just tell me where you want to go."

The hypnotizing circles of his fingers prevented her from answering. She hadn't been touched in so long. She'd only met Rafe once in person, convincing herself that their love was true because they seemed to understand one another so well in their long letters online.

But before him there'd been her college boyfriend. And he'd definitely needed directions in the touching department. A map would have been helpful, too.

She got quite a rush thinking Vito needed no instructions.

"Christine? You want to take this to my room? Your room?" His thumb and forefinger closed around her nipple, gently squeezing the taut peak. "Or do you want to return to your favorite showering place to fulfill my latest fantasy about you?"

"You think *you* have fantasies about the shower?" She closed her eyes as he leaned over the slight swell of her cleavage and allowed his warm breath to fan over her skin. "Try getting in that stall undressed and alone every night with the water pulsating over your skin—"

Vito placed a quieting finger over Christine's soft mouth, knowing he wouldn't survive any more fantasy description.

"You don't need to tell me. I've been picturing you wet and naked in there every night for three weeks." He tugged her out the back door of the garage, ready to live the scenario of all his recent dreams.

Mindful of the new sod she'd planted a few days ago, he pulled her through the yard, darting around the sprinklers spraying water in every direction. The water couldn't begin to cool him off now that she'd finally said yes. Besides, soon they would be much more wet.

Breathless and dripping, they hurried into the over-size workshop at the back of the property. Flicking on the low-wattage sconces Vito had laughed at his brother for making, he had to admit now they had their uses. The workshop had windows, but they were shuttered since no one used the shed anymore except for Christine.

Unable to wait any longer to get his hands on her, Vito locked the door behind them and then backed her into the heavy wooden barrier.

She tasted even better wet. He licked the sprinkler drops off her neck, savoring the clean taste of her skin and her softly fragranced hair. She smelled like green and growing things, vibrant and sweet.

And best of all she seemed to melt all over him every time he touched her. He had to admit that maybe waiting days and days for her to make up her mind about this had been a good thing. Whereas before she'd seemed kind of shy about the whole thing, now that she had made up her mind, she didn't hold a damn thing back.

"I can't wait," she whispered against his mouth, pulling at his clothes with frenzied fingers. "Not even another minute."

As her hands sailed down the front of his pants, he began to wonder if he could wait much longer, either.

"Are you tired?" He seized her questing fingers before they undid his belt.

She angled back to look at him in the moody yellow light from the wall sconces. "Do I seem tired to you?"

She rolled her hips against him for emphasis.

"No. Hell, no." He slid his hands under her sundress, splaying his fingers across her rib cage. "I just meant, maybe we can save the shower for round two since I think it's going to be a long night."

7

THIS WAS the best idea she'd ever had in her life.

Christine congratulated herself on her brilliance as she arched against Vito. His hands felt so good on her. His body made her ache for more of him. She leaned closer to him like a sun-seeking bloom. She needed his heat.

"I can guarantee there will be a round two." She stretched up on her toes to whisper in his ear, nipping the lobe with her teeth. "But I'm not waiting until then to get you in the shower."

Not when her fantasies about him all involved water streaming over that deep bronze skin of his. Sidling out of his arms she drew him toward the back of the workshop where the entrance to the outdoor shower waited.

Vito made a sound that could have been a groan or choked laughter. "What happened to the shy woman who's been avoiding me all month and took a week to decide whether or not to sleep with me?"

Christine paused beside her bag and withdrew two clean towels. "Shy? Didn't I tell you I was only avoiding you in an effort to staunch the flow of erotic fantasies?"

The surprise—and lust—in his eyes was priceless.

From a man who'd probably been with lots of women, his obvious desire for her sure pleased her. Made this attraction all the more special.

Not that she needed this to be special, she quickly reminded herself. Those types of thoughts could be downright dangerous. She was in this for the orgasm, damn it.

Feeling a bit mercenary as she dragged Vito's silk T-shirt up his chest, she couldn't suppress a sigh of pure female admiration.

"So you're not shy?" He helped her with his shirt by yanking it over his head and pitching it onto her duffel bag perched on the old desk.

"Definitely not. I just don't like to jump into anything without weighing the situation carefully." Her brothers Seth and Jesse would laugh at the idea of anyone thinking her shy. She'd been accused of a fierce independent streak before, and maybe a little stubbornness, but no one had ever pegged her for being too reserved.

A wicked smile curved Vito's lips.

"Good. Then you won't mind if I do this." With a flick of his fingers, her sundress lay in a rumpled pile at her feet. She stood before him clad in only her blue cotton bikini bottoms and a matching strapless bra.

His bold gaze raked over her, making her skin ache for his hands to follow the same path.

"A very good trick, Mr. Cesare." She backed closer to the wooden shower-stall door. "Is that what you learn over the course of seducing countless women across the globe?"

"Hardly." He reached for his belt buckle and whipped the length of leather out of the loops. "That's a trick I was only just inspired enough to try. Don't underestimate the appeal of seeing you naked."

Oh, he was good. Sexy as hell and charming the socks off her to boot. Her gaze moved unerringly to his hand as he carefully lowered his zipper. She licked her lips, her mouth suddenly too dry.

"I can see the appeal of naked," she agreed, unable to look away as he revealed black silk boxer shorts and stepped out of his pants.

Not before he removed a handful of condoms from the pocket, however. A big handful.

She counted one, two, three, four...

"*Five?* Are you always so optimistic?" She'd been counting on round two, but the thought of five rounds... Oh my. She felt a bit dizzy just contemplating it.

"Not optimistic. Inspired, remember?" One condom in hand, he stalked closer in the shadowy workshop, the wall sconces casting golden shadows over his skin. "And I can honestly say I've never been this inspired before."

"Oh." Her knees went a bit weak all over again. But before she could sway in the breeze like her fig tree, Vito's arms were around her, steadying her, propelling her out the door into the enclosed wooden shower stall with a clear view of the stars overhead.

The early evening air caressed her skin with welcome heat, chasing away the goose bumps Vito's hungry gaze had raised. In a flash his lips were on hers, his big hands skating over her skin to explore the curve of her waist. Her hips.

Head thrown back to his touch, she could have sworn she glimpsed a shooting star in the purple sky above before she closed her eyes. Amazingly, the tiny streak of light remained behind her lids even after she shut them tight.

"You won't regret saying yes," Vito murmured in her ear, his fingers sliding beneath one cup of her strapless bra. "I promise."

Christine sighed with pleasure as he palmed her breast. Reaching for the lever to turn on the water spray, she flicked the nozzle to hot.

"No regrets," she promised, determined to wrest only pleasure from her time with Vito.

Water blasted out of the showerhead, drenching them both where they stood. The cotton of her underwear clung to her wet skin as steam rose from their bodies up into the night sky.

Vito's hands were already tugging off her bra and panties, but not as quickly as she shoved off his black boxers. Their last articles of clothing were pitched over the wooden privacy wall to dry while they stepped directly into the shower spray.

The half moon just peeking above them didn't let her see enough of Vito's muscular body, but she rubbed her hands over every hard sinew to appreciate him fully. Rivulets of water streamed down his chest and she lapped at some with her tongue while she tracked the path of others with her fingertips.

Licking over damp skin and a flat male nipple, she tasted lower and lower until he stalled her just before she reached his abs, his hands tightening around her upper arms.

"Wait." Dragging her back up, his breathing was labored. Shallow. "That's definitely round two, honey. Listen to me on this one."

Smiling against his lips as she kissed him, she let him have his way this time. But then his hands slid over the slippery skin of her thighs, and her smile faded as need swamped her.

Fingers dancing a sultry trail through the curls between her thighs, he switched positions until he stood behind her, her body facing the shower stream head-on.

She wondered what he had in mind until he reached up to the showerhead with his other hand and adjusted the water flow lower. Lower.

To right *there*.

Her head lolled back against his shoulder as he spread her, exposing her to more and more of the relentless spray. The slow side of his fingers combined with the pulsating stream proved a heady combination.

A scream built in her throat just as Vito breathed in her ear.

"Come for me."

Her body erupted in sensual spasm, every muscle going taut with the orgasm that ripped through her. She couldn't hold back the cry of pure pleasure, but he covered her mouth with his hand just enough to keep her from waking the neighborhood.

She shuddered with the force of it, never having experienced anything close to the kind of pleasure he'd wrought.

And they hadn't even made love yet.

When the last aftershock faded away, she knew her legs would never hold her. Luckily, they didn't have to. Vito anchored her to him with one arm while he unearthed the condom from the soap dish and slid it on.

Bracing himself against the shower stall with one hand, he lifted her against him with the other. Still dazed from the surge of blood through her veins to all points south, Christine clung to him, content to let him take charge of her body since he obviously understood it a hell of a lot better than she ever had.

Only when he lifted her thigh high against his did she understand what he wanted. Her back against the stall wall, she held tight to his neck while she wrapped her legs around his waist. His strong arms supported her while she reached between them to guide him just where she wanted him.

With one roll of his hips he was pressing his way inside her, reawakening every nerve ending. He filled her completely as she held herself very still, waiting for her body to accommodate all of him.

And then the rhythm started.

More seductive than any pulsating stream of water, Vito moved inside her with the slow, steady motion of a man who knew how to pace himself.

Heart slogging in her chest, she cupped his chin in her palm, staring into his eyes in the moonlight as the cooling shower water poured over them. The heat in his gaze matched the gathering inferno inside her. She had only a split second to process all the dark emotion churning in his eyes before his mouth captured hers, his kiss tangling with hers to mirror the way he moved deep inside her.

Fingers sinking into his wet hair, she held onto him for dear life as the storm swelled inside her all over again. He brought her to the precipice of that mind-blowing moment again and again until at last he buried himself even deeper within her, sending her hurtling over the edge in one blinding instant.

His cry echoed hers this time, neither one of them possessing the wherewithal to hold back their shouts. Her heart pounded so loudly she couldn't even hear anything else. Her body was wracked with sensual shudders while Vito held her tightly against him.

She could have fallen asleep right there, sopping wet and exhausted, if he hadn't turned off the cold water raining down on them. Blinking herself out of the orgasmic bliss she'd just experienced, she slid her feet to the floor of the stall.

For a moment she thought maybe the fling was over when Vito walked out of the shower. But she only had a second to panic before he returned with the dry towels she'd left out.

She might have recovered her distance a little better if he'd just tossed her the towel and let her dry herself off. But he slung his around his neck and unfurled hers for her and then wrapped it—and his arms—around her. Slowly releasing her, he guided her back inside the workshop, holding the door for her as she ducked under his arm.

"We can sleep or we can start thinking about round two." He flicked a damp strand of hair from her eyes as he dried her off. "And just let me make it clear that whichever you choose, it's taking place in my bed."

Vito didn't mean to pressure her, but he couldn't let her go yet. Not after he'd just uncovered the wild side of his earthy goddess of home and hearth. What he'd perceived as shy had been her attempts to avoid him because she wanted him, too.

The revelation still rocked him as he stared down at her in the warm yellow light cast by the wall lamps.

He'd never pictured himself as a guy with a big Madonna complex, but maybe he hadn't realized a woman could possess such domestic instincts and still be so spontaneous in the shower. That didn't make him chauvinistic, right? Just clueless.

"Your bed?" The hesitation in Christine's voice jolted him back to the present.

"I've got four more condoms on deck, remember?" He let go of her long enough to wrap his towel around his waist. And then hesitated when he saw she wasn't getting dressed yet. "Would you prefer your bed?"

"It's not that." She hugged her towel tighter, looking way too damn vulnerable with her shoulders exposed, revealing the tan lines from the tank top she wore while she worked.

He expended considerable effort not to trace those pale lines with his finger. Even more effort not to lean down and trace them with his tongue.

"That'll set a record for the fastest fling ever if you're thinking about walking away already." And it would set an even bigger record for blows to the ego.

Shaking her head, she scooped up her sundress and tugged it over her head. Once it was on, she reached beneath the hem and yanked the towel out from underneath. A magic act of dressing that made sure he never got so much as a peek at her naked.

"I'm just wondering if we should draw certain boundaries regarding this...new facet of our relationship." She seemed to get distracted as she stared at his bare chest. Then tossing him his discarded T-shirt, she looked him in the eye. "You know, to help us maintain a sense of no expectations from one another?"

Dragging on the shirt, he nudged her toward the door. Maybe if he kept her distracted with talk until they got inside, he could maneuver her into his bedroom before she got too serious about the whole boundary idea.

"I thought we were allowed a few expectations." Holding the door for her, he peered around the dark backyard to make sure there weren't any lurking neighbors taking a late-night stroll.

"In a fling?" She sounded scandalized.

"Sure. I expect you to let me touch you all the time and you can expect me to give you as many orgasms as you want." He was only half kidding as he watched her walk, her hips swishing her skirt in a tantalizing rhythm.

"Maybe we should have initiated more discussion about this before we jumped into anything." She cast him a wary look while he hurried around her to open the door to the house.

"That would be a mistake." He ushered her into the kitchen where the night-light on the range hood cast a dull glow in an otherwise dark house. "If you start dissecting it and drawing too many parameters around it, then it won't feel like a fling anymore. I think a fling is supposed to be sort of spontaneous." Unable to resist those pale tan lines of hers any longer, he leaned forward to kiss one. "Fun."

"And I suppose you are an expert on the subject?"

Her clear blue eyes demanded the same honesty that she'd always given to him.

It caught him off guard.

"No." He backed up a step, wondering if he should have taken her up on the boundary-drawing idea while he had the chance. He hadn't expected to need them.

"You're *not* an expert?" She leaned against the kitchen counter, skepticism etched in every facet of her body language.

If this had been a media interview, he would have walked out. For the most part, he didn't care what conclusions other people drew about him. But he owed her better than that.

"I'll admit that I've waded into the waters of uncommitted relationships before." Far less often than she seemed to think, but he didn't know how to convince her of that. And worse, it worried him that he really wanted to convince her. "But I've never actually had a fling that successfully remained spontaneous and easy. Any time I've tried it, somehow it turns complicated by the end."

Ducking into the refrigerator, he pulled out her perpetually refilled container of lemonade and poured them both a glass.

He didn't know how she'd react to his past, but it seemed important to be straight with her. Handing her a drink, he waited to hear what she had to say and hoped like hell she wouldn't use this as an excuse to end things between them already.

Taking her lemonade from Vito's long, warm fingers, Christine wrapped her hands around the tall, chilly glass and tried to focus on the discussion at hand.

She should be glad that he'd been with other women like this, right? That meant he must be good at walking away once it was over.

Funny, the knowledge didn't seem to soothe her.

"Maybe your relationships turn complicated because women in your past haven't been honest with you about their expectations." Sipping the sweetly tart drink, she assured herself that wouldn't be the case for her and Vito. "You won't have that problem this time because I'm not nursing any secret desire to glom on to you or your fast-paced lifestyle. I'm happy in my new business venture and I've got big goals for myself that don't include any man."

So there.

She could almost hear the snippy sentiment behind the words. She hadn't meant to let the conversation ruffle her feathers, but even she could hear the defensiveness in her voice.

"What if I'm not the jet-setting player you seem to think I am?" His hazel eyes glittered dark and hot in the dim light of the kitchen. Vito's dark hair lay sleek and wet against his scalp, the strong features of his face rendered all the more prominent.

The desire to touch him lingered. If anything, her need for him had only intensified since the shower encounter.

She couldn't help but smile. "You drive a Ferrari. I don't think I can be too far off base on this."

"That's different. I happen to have fallen into my profession because I love cars." Placing his empty glass in the sink, he leaned on the counter beside her. Reminding her how vulnerable she was to his mere physical presence. "You wouldn't have thought I was such a jet-setter in my 1970s Chevelle that I drove while my brothers and sisters were growing up."

She tried to picture Mr. Continental in his silk T-shirt squiring around his troop of younger siblings while still so young himself. Her oldest brother Seth had taken on a ton of responsibilities after their father had walked out, but their mom had always been around to take care of the day-to-day stuff.

Vito had probably been about the same age as her or maybe a little younger when he'd stepped into the shoes of a parent. Could she have taken on that kind of challenge successfully? The notion sobered her when she considered all the trouble she was having just getting a business off the ground.

"How did you support all your siblings? Did you work?"

Rolling his eyes, he leaned away from the kitchen counter and started going through the cabinets as if searching for something.

"Hell, yeah, I worked. But since I hadn't even finished my own college degree at the time, I just took over my father's cabinetry business. My brother Renzo loves that kind of stuff, but I was never cut out for spending the whole day with a saw in hand. Or a measuring tape."

Digging through the cabinets, he unearthed a box of sugar cookies and set a stack in front of each of them.

Munching a cookie since she wasn't getting what she really craved, Christine tried to imagine what it would be like to be stuck laboring in an unwanted job.

"It's important to love your work." Which accounted for why she was so determined to make her landscaping business successful. Since her starry-eyed dreams of romance had failed to lead to any kind of real relationship, her work was her whole life.

"You're not kidding. To this day, the smell of sawdust makes me cranky. But at the time, I just did what I had to do."

Christine studied him in the intimate quiet of the half-dark kitchen, admiring him for the sacrifices he'd made for his family. Maybe he wasn't quite the globe-trotting player she'd first thought. After raising his siblings at such a young age, the guy surely deserved some time to indulge himself however he saw fit.

But even as the realization made her understand his need to drive fast cars and live his dreams of racing, she didn't feel quite so magnanimous about his other forays into uncommitted relationships. Since when did having a few responsibilities in life excuse a man from being faithful?

As much as both of her brothers had driven her crazy

growing up, she had to admire their staunch commitment to their wives. Even her brother Jesse, who'd been a notorious bad boy, had finally seen the wisdom of staying with one woman.

Frowning, she stared across the countertop at Vito. "I'm not suggesting it's any of my business or anything, but I'm curious about what you've got against relationships. Is it too hard to stay faithful in your line of work? Women throw themselves at your feet?"

"Hell, no." He readjusted the towel still slung around his hips. "Show me someone who uses their career as an excuse to cheat and I'll show you someone who doesn't ever deserve to be married. I'm just not ready to get serious with anyone because I've been having too much fun catching up on all the stuff I missed out on when I was younger. I wouldn't ever want to mislead anyone."

For a moment, her inner romantic let out another heartfelt sigh that Vito was the kind of guy who still believed in the sanctity of a committed relationship even if he didn't opt to have one himself. And then she woke up and heard the message behind his words.

He didn't want to mislead anyone.

Meaning her. He didn't want her to get any wrong ideas about them because he wasn't ready to be serious about anyone.

Swilling down the rest of her lemonade, she set the glass on the counter with a thud.

"Well you don't need to worry about that with me.

I've got the ground rules memorized. Fun. Spontaneous. And at the end of my time here, we both walk away happy." And nobody gets hurt, damn it.

She didn't need to worry about his concerns because she wasn't going to be one of those women in his life who couldn't let go. No matter how phenomenal the sex was, she wasn't ready for a real relationship in her life, either. She had a career to get off the ground and a new cynical streak to balance out the damn romantic lunatic who'd been running her life before Rafe.

Now she could handle a guy like Vito Cesare without getting burned. This fling would be a success.

"Excellent." Brushing the crumbs from their cookies into the sink, he straightened. "So what do you think, Christine? Are you bailing on me already or do I get to haul you off to my lair and have my wicked way with you again?"

8

SHE'D said yes.

Vito couldn't believe how willing Christine had been to toss aside the more traditional conventions of romance simply to explore the chemistry between them.

A week later he made her breakfast while she slept a few extra hours. A fair trade considering he'd kept her up half the night, unable to get enough of her. The woman was amazing, by turns sexy and sweet. Sometimes she tantalized him with surprise caresses under the table at dinner or while he talked on the phone to his slew of Italian relatives who needed directions to the house since they would all be arriving for the wedding next week.

Other times she floored him with how generous she could be, delivering all of Mrs. Kowolski's specialty orders one day when the neighbor's truck broke down. And just last night Christine had spent two hours helping Mrs. Hollenbeck rearrange a flower bed near her front door to better showcase the new porch she'd added on to her house.

Carefully folding his first attempt at an omelette in half, Vito double-checked the cookbook instructions to be sure he had it right. He'd need about six more ome-lettes if she was half as hungry as him. Their shared late nights were giving him a hell of an appetite lately.

He was rooting around the refrigerator for more eggs when his phone rang.

"Hello?" Cradling the receiver against his shoulder, he spied another dozen behind a mountain of fresh lem-ons.

"Hey *pisan*." His sister Giselle's voice rolled across the line, her normally suppressed Italian accent coming across full steam now that she'd taken up temporary residence in Naples while her journalist fiancé worked on a story nearby. "I'm starting to panic about planning the whole wedding from afar. Please tell me you're tak-ing care of getting the house ready so I don't have to worry about that once I get in next week?"

"I've got the house covered. And thanks to Giuseppe hiring the landscaper, the property is going to look bet-ter than it ever has. All the neighbors keep dropping by to get ideas for their yards."

Although he'd be willing to bet Mrs. Hollenbeck's teenage son had only dropped by to get a better look at Christine's legs.

"Giuseppe swears he's found your mate for life, you know." Giselle giggled as she whispered to someone on the other end of the phone, then turned her full atten-tion back to Vito again. "He kept Aunt Sophia on the phone for half an hour last night raving about the gar-dener he'd hired. Christine, right?"

Sliding his omelette out of the skillet and onto a plate to keep warm in the oven, Vito debated how to answer his sister without raising suspicions or giving credence to Giuseppe's matchmaking efforts.

"She's really talented." He'd just keep his comments focused on her professional skills. No need for anyone to know she'd rocked his world on every possible personal level, too.

"Giuseppe says she's also a total babe."

"I'm not even going there, so don't ask." Cracking more eggs into a bowl, he peered down the hallway toward Christine's bedroom. She had embraced the idea of a tryst in the shower and a quickie on the dining room table, but she'd drawn the line at spending the whole night in his bed. Every night before dawn she slipped from his room to seek the privacy of her own.

"Oh, good. If you're not interested in her, I'm sure Marco will be. He was just saying the other night he needs a date."

Vito spilled an egg on the floor. "Damn it, Giselle, I know what you're trying to do and it won't work. Christine is about ten times more mature than Marco." Even if she *was* closer in age to his youngest brother than him. Something about Christine's down-to-earth practicality made the age difference between her and Vito irrelevant.

"No need to be prickly about it. I don't have to introduce her to anyone if you don't want me to. It just seemed a shame to let a woman who's talented *and* a total babe slip away."

"I'm in the middle of breakfast here, sis." It took a great deal of effort to talk through clenched teeth. "Did you want anything or can I get back to my omelette now?"

Out of the corner of his eye he spied a flash of yellow. Turning, he found Christine at his elbow, helping herself to a juice glass in the cupboard.

He stared at her, determined to cut his sister off before Christine could leave the kitchen.

Giselle's voice sounded in his ear over the phone line. "As the matter of fact, I wanted to talk to Christine about the landscaping and run a few ideas for the wedding photos by her. Is she around?"

Damn. He couldn't very well keep Giselle from making her plans. Even if she was a pain in the neck, she was still his sister and he'd been ready to marry her off ever since he caught her necking in the driveway with Billy Spears.

"Yeah, she's here."

"Oh, and Vito?"

"What?"

"You do realize you have to invite her to the wedding after she's done so much hard work for me, right?"

He refused to argue with her because good manners said she had a point. And he sure as hell wasn't going to admit to toying with the idea of inviting her as his personal guest anyhow.

"I know. Hang on a minute." He passed the phone to Christine and tried not to eavesdrop while he finished making breakfast. Actually, it was pretty damn easy not to eavesdrop since his sister did ninety-nine percent of the talking while Christine nodded a lot and agreed.

By the time she was finished, he had the table set with their eggs and toast.

"So?" He couldn't deny being a little curious about what had taken place. Especially since Giselle seemed as ready to play Cupid as their uncle—even if it involved matching Christine up with someone else.

A fact which seriously compromised his appetite.

"Your sister just wants me to test out a few locations for photos." She clicked off the phone and flipped her napkin into her lap. "Thank you for making breakfast, by the way. It smells fantastic."

"You're welcome." He slid into his seat at the table. "What do you mean 'test out locations'? The gardens are almost finished. She can't possibly expect you to swap anything around at this point, can she?"

"Apparently she just wants us to take a few digital photos at late afternoon so she can see how the light will look in a few different spots around the yard." Christine shrugged. "Not a big deal. She said you have a camera?"

Vito wondered what the catch was. Was Giselle just that curious to see Christine? "We've got one some-where."

"And it has a timer?" She asked between bites of omelette.

"A timer?"

"If she's testing out locations for her wedding photos, I'm sure she'd like to see two people in each shot to give her a better preview."

"Ahh."

"What, 'ahh'?"

"She's joined forces with Uncle Giuseppe to coerce the two of us to do things together. Don't you see?" Damn but his family was transparent.

"I'm afraid I don't." Christine cleaned her plate and then stole two more bites of omelette off his plate. "She said she wants a spot with lots of flowers or greenery in the background. It made perfect sense to me."

Vito shoved his plate closer to her so they could share the last of the eggs. "This week we need to pose for bogus photos together. By next week she'll be expecting us to announce our engagement. It's all very diabolical."

Standing, she carried her plate to the dishwasher. "Did it ever occur to you that maybe you're not as surrounded by scheming matchmakers as you seem to believe? Frankly, I'm less inclined to believe your sister is diabolical and more inclined to believe you're just a tiny bit paranoid about the possibility of losing your single-guy lifestyle."

"Paranoid?" Where did she get that from? "You don't know my family."

"Maybe not. But just the same, let me reassure you again—you don't have a thing to worry about when it comes to me." She rinsed out the frying pan and put it in the sink. "I'll be out of here by the time your sister marches down the aisle and you can go back to being the Cesare family's most eligible bachelor."

Drying off her hands, she headed for the kitchen door to start her day in the gardens, her long, tanned legs making his mouth water.

"Wait." He reached over her head to keep the door shut. Needing her to stay with him for a few more minutes. Hours. Did she have to be so committed to this damn job for his uncle?

He inhaled her flowery fragrance as he leaned in for a quick taste of her neck. Her pulse pounded fast and furious beneath his lips.

"What?" Her voice sounded throaty and breathless, just the way he liked it. But her body was still taut, rigid. Ready to get to her work outside that was so damn important to her.

"Don't go yet." He couldn't think how to convince her to stay a little longer, so he licked his way up her throat. Tugged on her lower lip.

"Vito, I can't get behind on this job." She sounded as disappointed as he was, her breath coming in little gasps as he skimmed his hand over her hip.

Hell. He'd have her later. When he could take as many hours as he wanted to explore every last inch of her.

"Vito?" She stared at him now, her lips swollen from his kiss while she waited to see what he wanted.

And since he wasn't going to admit to attempted seduction over the breakfast table he thought fast. Remembered Giselle would be pissed if he didn't invite Christine to the wedding soon, right?

Better now than never. After a week of her keeping plenty of boundaries in place despite the fling, he realized he wanted something more from her anyway. Maybe he'd find out what if he spent a little more time with her when they weren't both horizontal.

There were sexy-as-hell spots of color in her cheeks, her shallow breaths making her chest rise and fall in a way that couldn't help but catch his eye. Still, he forced himself not to start undressing her then and there. Instead, he forced words from his mouth.

"I don't want you to leave before the wedding."

CHRISTINE was obviously experiencing some form of sex-crazed dementia because there's no way determined bachelor Vito Cesare had just asked her to stick around for his sister's nuptials.

Deciding that playing ignorant and waiting for him to spell out what he meant would be the least embarrassing course of action, she leaned against the door and stared up at him in the sunny kitchen.

"What do you mean?" She licked her lips and caught his flavor still lingering on her mouth.

"I mean I'd like to you to stay a little longer and go to

Giselle's wedding with me in two weeks." His hazel eyes darkened to golden brown as he stared down at her, his voice going soft and low.

Her heart turned over in her chest at his invitation, his words appealing to every romantic bone in her body. Still, she hesitated.

By agreeing to a fling with Vito she'd somehow signed on for the most physically intense, sensually satisfying week of her whole life. And while she'd loved every minute of uncovering her inner sex goddess, she'd also begun to realize that she couldn't undertake all that hot and steamy sex without engaging her emotions. Every night as she lay next to Vito, whether it be strewn over the living-room floor or curled securely beside him in bed, she'd started feeling those old pangs of romanticism, that deep-seated longing for a real family complete with smiling kids, an overzealous golden retriever and neighbors who baked cookies for each other on special occasions.

She'd been fighting those feelings tooth and nail every day, but she didn't stand a chance of battling them if Vito did things like invite her to attend family celebrations with him.

"I don't know." She didn't want her heart broken. A fate that was assured if she started feeling all mushy inside about a certain avowed bachelor.

She probably would have been better off forgetting about planting her bird of paradise flowers today and just enjoying the way he'd been touching her earlier. Right now she could be experiencing multiple Os instead of battling a major attack of romance.

"Attending a wedding together doesn't sound like an appropriate activity for people having a fling, does it?" She was already beginning to wonder how she'd survive the next two weeks with Vito, let alone if their time together was capped off by orange blossoms and "Here Comes the Bride."

Way to stab a romantic in the heart.

He seemed to appreciate her point because he nodded slowly as if deep in thought. "You're right. But Giselle really wants you there after you've worked so hard to make her big day special."

"I'm sure I can think of some excuse. We can say I contracted food poisoning or something equally hideous." It beat being heartsick, that was for sure.

Vito continued as if he hadn't heard her. "Besides, if you're not there, I'll have to wade through a hundred people asking me when I'm going to settle down. If you go with me, everyone will just smile at us and leave us alone."

She could see his reasoning. But it still managed to sting just a little when she'd sort of hoped he wanted to go with her for more personal reasons.

"Are you suggesting you'd like me to do this as a favor?" Because that could sway her. If she based a decision on what was best for her, she'd have to decline.

But Vito had just made her breakfast. And he'd spent two hours yesterday helping her figure out how to reprogram the complex sprinkler system she'd installed for the yard. Since she'd bought it on clearance because of the bargain rate she'd given Giuseppe, the system didn't come with any instruction manual and it turned out Vito had a real talent for computerized gizmos. Despite his penchant for race cars and fast living, he was a really nice—and, it seemed, supersmart—guy.

"Depends." He leaned a shoulder against the door, his big body still blocking her exit. "Would you consider that a breach of friendship if I did?"

She considered the question and had to admire that he'd bothered to check with her first.

"No. I guess I wouldn't."

He grinned. "Then I'm asking. Please go with me, Christine."

Ignoring the erratic beat of her heart, she stifled that damn romantic streak of hers and nodded. "I'll go with you."

"Thank you." For a moment, his eyes locked on hers, inciting the tingling warmth in her veins that usually preceded a kiss. But then he stepped away from the door to clear her path. "I'll bring out the camera this afternoon so we can take care of those photos my sister wants."

Nodding, Christine hurried out the door to get away from the intimacy of shared breakfasts and shared wedding plans. They were proving even more dangerous than shared kisses.

And at this rate, her heart would be lucky to survive their fling.

VITO FELT damn lucky when it started to rain later that day.

And it wasn't just any rain. This was a southern Florida rain. A no-holds-barred, subtropical downpour that made it impossible to shoot photos and even made it impossible for ever-industrious Christine Chandler to continue working outside.

Shutting down his computer program for designing custom racetracks, Vito slid into his shoes and sprinted outside to help her put her tools away. The rain was so loud she had to shout instructions to him for covering up a flat full of new annuals she was planting just for the wedding.

By the time they finished stowing the tools in the workshop, they were drenched. Christine's navy-and-white T-shirt with the words All Natural scrawled across the front clung to her curves invitingly. Her chin-length hair molded to her scalp as water streamed from the strands down her neck.

She stood in the open doorway of the workshop and stared at the house through the sheeting rain. "You ready to make a run for it?"

Christine watched Vito peer around the wooden building, mostly vacant except for garden tools and the utilitarian desk at the back bearing her duffel bag. Then he looked at her with a wicked gleam in his eyes.

"It's not raining in here."

"There are also no blankets to play tent with and no bed to burrow in." She shivered—partly from the cold but mostly at the thought of bedroom games with Vito. Propping the door open with a wooden block, she turned to him. "I vote we make a run for it."

His hand slid around hers and before she knew it, he had her in his arms. "If I play tent with you, do you think this could be the day you spend the whole night in my bed?"

Thunder rumbled ominously in the distance and she could have sworn the sky outside the half-open door went a few shades darker.

"I don't know about that." Actually she did know about that, and it was a bad, bad idea. But it was difficult to remember why when her hips were fitted up against his this way, her breasts molded to that hard male chest of his.

He caught a drop of water on her cheek with his thumb. "This fling didn't pull down many barriers for you, did it?"

"And who are you to complain, Mr. Spontaneous?" She kept her words light as she smiled, unwilling to reveal any more of herself to this man who knew too much already. "The fling made the barrier of our clothes go away." She splayed her fingers along the solid muscle of his abs. "That ought to count for something."

He sucked in a sharp breath as her finger dipped below the waist of his shorts. "It counts for a hell of a lot."

"Then there's no need to push for more since you told me yourself you want to keep things uncomplicated." She feathered kisses across his chest and the damp cotton T-shirt that covered him.

She'd hemmed and hawed for nearly a week over whether to have a fling in the first place. He couldn't change the ground rules on her now.

He cupped her chin in his hand, tipping her head to look at him. "Then you don't have to spend the whole night in my bed. But please know that I want you there."

The suppressed dreamy sigh whistled through her with gale force, making her knees weak with want. If she stared into those expressive hazel eyes of his any longer she would fall right inside.

The storm blowing outside looked positively tame compared to the unwanted emotional firestorm blazing through her. Better to brave the raindrops today than risk teardrops at a later date. She was getting out of the workshop before she made any promises she couldn't keep.

"I'll keep that in mind." She called up a smile to diffuse the lingering sense of want inside her. Nodding toward the open door and the downpour outside, she winked. "You ready to race, hotshot?"

Vito wasn't used to being last out of the gate, but as he watched Christine race through the downpour, he consoled himself that at least he knew how to pace himself. She might be a novice at the whole racing game, but he had the feeling he could convince her of the merits of taking her time once he got her inside.

Fueled by her challenge and the heat in her eyes, he closed the workshop door behind him and then made tracks across the new, lush green sod toward the house.

But when he reached the door to the kitchen and shut out the wind and rain, she was nowhere in sight. The house was quiet. Still.

For a moment he wondered what this summer would have been like here without her. His days would have been filled with running errands for Giselle and tweaking his rudimentary attempts at software for a racing game. And, as much as he loved his sister and enjoyed messing around on the computer, he had to admit he would have been bored out of his mind in no time.

As he slid off his shoes and dried his face on a clean towel, he spied Christine's wet boots parked on the green rug by the door. Obviously she'd come in the house.

She was just hiding.

Or maybe lying in wait for him.

Anticipation fired through his blood at the thought of her stretched out in his bed, naked and waiting for him. Tossing the towel on the counter, he stalked through the house. Without a doubt, this was his best trip home ever.

He listened for telltale signs of movement outside her

closed bedroom door but could only hear his own heart pumping with aggressive force. All else remained still. Bypassing her door for his, again he listened. Waited.

Nothing.

He'd lose his mind if he didn't find her soon. Foregoing all attempts at stealth, he barged into his room.

Found her.

She was naked all right, but she wasn't draped over his bed like a centerfold. She was tucked under his covers and curled up tight, with only her bare shoulder peeking out of the blankets to clue him into her Lady Godiva state.

"Took you long enough," she taunted from her reclined position. Her damp hair looked all the darker against the crisp white pillowcase. "I was beginning to think maybe you needed more incentive."

Her wicked grin told him she knew damn well she'd lured him here.

Stripping off his shirt, he tossed the damp fabric into a heap on the floor near her discarded clothes.

"I had plenty of incentive watching you frolic around the yard in a wet T-shirt."

"I was not frolicking." She propped herself up on an elbow in the bed, the blankets slipping dangerously low on her breasts.

By accident? Or by design?

He was beginning to appreciate that no matter how much she seemed like the home-and-hearth type with her green thumb and penchant for helping out all his neighbors, she hid a sensuous streak a mile wide. And for some reason, the fact that she kept her wild side under wraps, revealed to him alone, was ten times more appealing than if she paraded around in stilettos and French lingerie. He liked the contrast of her leather work boots with a come-hither stare.

"Then how about some frolicking now?" He ditched his shorts before stretching out over her, his body already humming with need. "It sounded like you had some games in mind involving a bed and a few blankets, and here we are."

Her scent drifted up to him, clean and rain-washed. Her cheeks were flushed pink from their mad dash outside, her lips soft and beckoning in the dim light filtering through the windows from the stormy sky.

She wound her arms around his neck, tugging him closer. "If I can't get any work done today, then I might as well play."

Something sweet and honest and real flashed in her blue eyes before she closed them, shutting him out of whatever she was feeling.

Just as well, he thought, given that he'd be leaving town after the wedding and most likely would never see Christine Chandler again. But even as the thought formed in his head he hated it. Hated the idea of not seeing her. Regretted not giving her the kind of wine-and-roses fling she deserved.

Promising himself he'd at least make their last two weeks together the best they could be, Vito slanted his mouth over hers. Tasting the hot sweetness of her, he savored the way she moaned in the back of her throat. The way she speared her fingers into his hair to draw him deeper. Closer.

Desire already flooding his veins, he inched down the covers between them. He still wanted to take his time tonight, lavish every square inch of her with pleasure. But first he needed to feel her naked against him.

Brushing the thermal blanket aside, his fingers were just sweeping over the lush curve of her breast when a noise sounded in the back of his brain.

No. A noise sounded in the hallway.

His hands went still as he waited. Listened.

Until a boisterous male voice boomed from down the hallway.

"Hey Vito! Is this any way to greet your favorite uncle?"

9

"THIS CAN'T be happening." Christine lay back on the bed and wished she could bury her head in the pillows.

She knew that voice. And she knew the energetic, jovial man attached to it.

She just didn't care to see him right now, when she had been ready to spend hour after blissful hour tangling limbs with the sexiest man she'd ever met.

"I can get rid of him." Vito shoved himself off the bed, tugging the covers over her as he went. Then he shouted through the closed door. "Be there in a minute, Uncle Giuseppe."

Tossing the sheet aside, she grabbed her wet clothes. "That's okay. I feel unprofessional enough having a fling with the boss's nephew. I sure don't want to avoid my employer when he shows up to check my progress."

Her stomach knotted at the thought of being perceived as unprofessional. She'd worked so hard to make the property exceed Giuseppe's expectations, she couldn't stand the thought of blowing it because she'd exercised poor judgment in sleeping with Vito.

"Trust me, he's not here to check your progress."

Vito shot her a dark look as he put on a dry T-shirt and then tossed her one, too. "I know you don't want to hear it, Christine, but he's most likely here to check out *mine.*"

Staring down at the blue shirt stamped with a Grand Prix racing logo he'd given her, she tried to follow that logic and failed.

Perhaps her blank look said as much.

"He probably wants to see if I'm making any inroads with you." Smoothing the blankets on the mattress like a teenager caught with his girlfriend, he shoved their discarded clothes under the bed. "Remember? I think half his motive was to get us together."

"Well, he sure succeeded there, didn't he?" Suddenly miffed with herself for falling so predictably into Vito's bed, she shrugged her way into the dry shirt and dragged her fingers through her damp, tousled locks. "I can't see the point in hiding it. I've done a kick-ass job on the yard, so it's not like I've been slacking off on my responsibilities to steal quickies with you."

Giuseppe's voice boomed through the door again. "Vito?"

"Damn." Vito reached behind her neck to tuck the tag in on the back of her shirt. "He'd never think that, Christine. But you don't need to deal with him right now if you don't want."

"I'm ready." Thankfully she sounded more confident than she felt. "Let's go."

Nodding, he planted a kiss on her forehead and pulled open the door.

Giuseppe stood in the hallway, possibly eavesdropping and not looking repentant in the least. A grin split his face, his white teeth a bright contrast to his dark olive skin. His close-cropped dark hair was thinning slightly on top, but otherwise he showed little sign of his age.

Dressed in tan cargo shorts and a neat leather belt, his green polo shirt tucked and pressed, Christine would have never pegged him for a mechanic. But then again, she sort of hoped she didn't go around looking as if she played in dirt for a living.

But Giuseppe Donzinetti's clothes were so crisp he could have just stepped out of a Gap ad.

"Bon giorno!" He wrapped Vito in a bear hug before he kissed his cheek and clapped his back. "You're finally home where you should be."

Whatever Vito said in response was drowned out by the bear hug Giuseppe turned on her.

"And now you're practically family." He let her go after a hard squeeze. Thankfully, he skipped the back-clapping which had looked borderline painful. "My nephew is a nice guy once you get him away from all his cars and his fancy parties. I work on cars for a living, and even *I* get tired of talking about cars with him sometimes. But you like him, eh?"

Hoping a smile would suffice for an answer, she wondered why she hadn't simply taken Vito's advice and hidden in the bedroom. Much, much better idea. The "practically family" comment had not only caught her off guard, it also called to her romantic side with all the subtlety of a foghorn.

Coming to her rescue, Vito dropped an arm around his uncle's shoulders and guided him toward the dining room. "Christine doesn't want to talk about me. I hope you realize how hard she's had to work to get the landscaping finished in time for the wedding. She only quit early today because of the rain."

As Giuseppe took a seat at the table, he looked genuinely worried as he glanced back at her. "I didn't mean for you to spend all your time working this summer."

"I'm enjoying it, actually." Which was true. Even when she'd been deep in the labor-intensive portion of the project she'd had fun planning the lawn and gardens to show off the house to its best advantage while providing tranquil areas to relax or entertain. "I love what I do."

The doorbell rang before she could launch into her spiel about all she'd accomplished on the property. She couldn't stand to have Giuseppe think for a minute that she might be slacking on her part of the bargain.

Vito excused himself to answer the door while she started pointing out the window to a few of the most obvious changes in the yard.

Half listening to Christine talk about fire bushes and fig trees, Vito squinted out the frosted-glass windowpane in the kitchen door for a hint of who else had arrived. He really hoped the rest of his relatives would wait a few more days before descending on him since Christine looked shell-shocked enough just trying to handle Giuseppe.

As he pulled open the door, however, he realized he had nothing to worry about. Mrs. Kowolski stood on his doorstep, her arms loaded down with fancy white boxes bearing the logo for her catering company.

"I don't mean to intrude." She thrust her pile of boxes into Vito's arms and stepped inside. "But since I knew you were expecting a lot of company in the next two weeks I thought you might be able to use some extra sweets for your guests."

"Sweets?" From the dining room, Giuseppe's voice halted Christine's running monologue about the yard.

His head bobbed into view a moment later, Christine shadowing him as they entered the kitchen like sugar-crazed zombies following the scent of almond and lemon.

"Hi, Mary Jo," Christine called when Giuseppe remained uncharacteristically silent. "You are a goddess. All those are for us?"

"And your guests," Mrs. K. reminded her, gaze fastened on Uncle Giuseppe. "Have they started arriving already?"

Staggering under the unwieldy stack of boxes, Vito lowered them onto the kitchen counter while Christine made the introductions. By the time he turned back to thank his neighbor, the local catering maven was edging her way back out the door, her cheeks pink.

"Good luck with the wedding preparation," she called hastily over her shoulder. "I'll stop by next week to see if you need anything else."

What had he missed? Mrs. K. had never left a friend's house that fast in all her life. She hadn't told a single story about the rowdy Cesare clan in their youth.

He might have been tempted to ask Christine what the heck was going on, but when he turned to her, she had big grin on her face.

"You like her, eh?" She winked at Giuseppe while his uncle craned his neck to stare out the frosted-glass windowpane at the departing figure.

Ah. He might not have a clue about romance, but somehow Christine had seen the signs of attraction between the two widowers.

"Mary Jo Kowolski lost her husband at least three years ago," Vito offered, all too willing to join Christine in turning the tables on his uncle's matchmaking efforts. He'd never get her back into his bed with Giuseppe around. "She's been running a catering business by herself ever since. I would have thought you'd have run into her before now."

Giuseppe peered into the stack of catering boxes now that Mary Jo's van had driven out of sight. "I would have remembered her." Taking a bite of a frosted gingersnap, he sighed with pleasure. "And I would never forget a woman who baked like that."

"Too bad she's been having so many problems with her delivery van." Christine winked at Vito behind Giuseppe's back as she dived into a box of shortbread cookies. "I had to help her make all her rounds with my pickup truck last week."

His uncle's eyes widened. "I'm a mechanic. Maybe I could help."

"I'm sure she'd be really grateful. And she'll probably be around tomorrow morning if you had time to—"

"I'll stop by." He smoothed the collar on his shirt. "Just to be neighborly, of course."

"Of course." Vito stifled a grin as he thought about the Giuseppe-free hours he could enjoy with Christine tomorrow morning. Maybe if his uncle was busy dodging Cupid's arrows himself, he wouldn't have time to fling so many at other people. "Do you need me to help you bring your bags in, Giuseppe? I assume you're going to stay here for the wedding, aren't you?"

Straightening, Giuseppe looked mortally offended. "And get in the way of true love?"

Was it Vito's imagination, or did Christine's face turn a few shades paler?

"This is the bride's childhood home," he explained, a mischievous twinkle in his brown eyes. "I'm sure she'll want to stay in her old home with her fiancé. I've already booked two weeks at a bed and breakfast near the water."

Vito wondered if Christine would be checking out of the Cesare house soon, too. Once she realized she'd be dodging the relentless efforts of matchmaking Italians for two weeks, she might gladly hightail her way out of his life for the solitude of a Motel 6.

And despite his fears about their relationship getting too complicated, Vito found himself surprisingly reluctant to let her go—whether it be tomorrow or two weeks from now.

He didn't have time to worry about it now, however, since Uncle Giuseppe was wrapping his big arms around both of them and drawing them all close in a family hug.

"But for now, we eat!" He shouted the last words like a call to arms. Eating was serious business for many old-school Italians, and Giuseppe Donzinetti in particular. "Get your umbrellas, kids. Dinner's on me."

FOUR DAYS LATER, Christine thought she'd lose her mind if even one more relative knocked on Vito's door.

After Giuseppe arrived in town, a steady stream of wedding guests insinuated themselves into the Cesare household on a daily basis, trampling her sod with high-heeled pumps, assuring her she didn't need to spend so much time working in the garden and enthusing over what a great couple she and Vito made. And just when she thought life couldn't conspire against her any more, fate sent her a sunny day and a frantic phone call from the bride asking about her test photos.

Now, as Christine readied her scarlet milkweed flowers for their close-up under the glaring rays of the late-afternoon sun, she wondered how she could possibly pose for a picture with Vito so close to her and refrain from tearing off his clothes.

"It looks *bellisimo*, Christina." Uncle Giuseppe called to her from his perch on one of the new faux stone benches she'd installed around the gardens. "All I need in the picture now is a couple glowing with the blush of young love."

Stifling the urge to roll her eyes as she finished adjusting a wayward branch of flowers, she didn't have the heart to tell Giuseppe that any glow she might have was a direct result of frustrated lust and not remotely related to love. She and Vito had barely gotten within kissing distance of one another in the past four days thanks to international flights arriving at the airport at all hours of the day and night.

Even after Vito finished playing host to his seemingly endless extended family during the day, he would wait for hours at the airport in the middle of the night for delayed flights to arrive so he could drive more guests to their respective hotels. Or else he'd drive them back to the Cesare house for a night or two until the party in question got wind of Giuseppe's matchmaking scheme, and then they'd make excuses about how they'd always wanted to stay at the Coral Gables Quality Inn.

From behind her, she heard Vito's voice. "You'd better behave, Uncle Giuseppe, or I'll have to go tell Mrs. K. you only fixed her van so she would invite you to dinner one of these nights."

Threats concerning Mary Jo Kowolski were the only weapon that seemed to help.

"No need to sell me out, Vito." Giuseppe smoothed a hand over his thinning dark hair and cast a covert glance at Mary Jo's house with its wide, inviting porches.

He'd been transparently smitten with Vito's neighbor from the moment she'd stepped into the Cesare kitchen bearing cookies. For four days straight he'd been asking questions about Mary Jo and stealing surreptitious peeks out the window toward her house, but he had yet to do more than smile politely at her and offer some mechanical help.

For a guy who made romantic meddling his number-one hobby, he sure didn't seem to have a clue how to manage his own love life.

Speaking of which, if she didn't start taking some initiative with her own, Giuseppe's high-handed approach would send Vito screaming back to Europe long before she got her fill of kisses. And more.

She took a deep breath and decided to take matters into her own hands.

"Okay, I'm ready. The plants are ready." Better that she be the one in control of this situation than to have Giuseppe scripting an awkward pose between her and Vito. "Let's get the pictures over with so I can finish up my last round of pesticide spraying before the wedding. Vito, are you ready?"

Her gaze flashed to his, hoping he'd come along for

the ride with her on this one. She'd far rather get the photo right the first time than to have Giuseppe debate with them all afternoon about how they should get closer. Kiss each other. Yadda, yadda, yadda.

They'd do it right the first time and then they'd be off the hook to go do their own things today. Which—considering the luck she and Vito had been having this week—would probably involve Vito chauffeuring his aunts around to the local shopping venues so they could find dresses to wear to all the wedding activities Giselle and her fiancé had planned.

"Hell, yes, I'm ready." He was near enough to her that only she heard his words as Giuseppe cleaned the lens of the camera with a corner of his knit polo shirt.

Vito stepped closer still, joining her under the natural arch of flowers made by an old honeysuckle vine and a slew of new orange, red and yellow plantings. The vibrant colors would attract plenty of hummingbirds for years to come, and the warm tones would complement the bride's Italian-American complexion. Christine had seen pictures of Giselle around the Cesare house and—no surprise since she was Vito's sister—she was beautiful.

"Then let's get this over with before we spontaneously combust, okay?" Christine whispered under her breath, mindful of Giuseppe testing camera angles a few feet away from them.

"Too late." Vito spoke through the clenched teeth of his camera-ready smile while his hand slid around her back. He tucked her close to his side as they faced the camera. "I'm combusting on a nightly basis while I lie awake and wish I could be in your bed."

Christine could feel her fake camera smile turn into the real thing. "Oh, really? Do tell, Mr. Cesare. I like to think I'm not the only one burning up every night."

Giuseppe must have found an angle he liked because he called to them over the camera.

"Okay, kids, we're ready to shoot. No more talking." He frowned as he stared at them over the lens. "And no more goofy grins. You've just gotten married, remember? You're in looove."

He gave the last work about six syllables too many.

Vito dutifully turned toward Christine. "I think you're taking your camera work a little too seriously over there, old man."

"Nothing's too good for my niece's wedding." Giuseppe shook a stern finger at them both although his eyes remained lit with mischief. "And you'd do well to remember how important weddings are for family, eh? Without the wedding, there is no family, no crazy relatives to indulge and no more fun. Trust me, weddings are good. Family is even better."

Christine didn't have to worry about removing her goofy grin. It came sliding off all on its own at the first mention of weddings and family. Half of her wanted to embrace Vito's uncle in a big hug as a fellow romantic, but the other half of her—the half that was trying very hard to gag her dreamy impulses—needed to plug her ears at his ardent defense of love and marriage.

Of course, it didn't help that Vito's broad hand rested on the curve of her waist, his pinky straying down to her hip and tantalizing her with how awesome it would be to combine all that love and marriage stuff with the heady sensuality she'd discovered in Vito's arms.

Somewhere in the back of her mind she heard Giuseppe shout, *"Si, si!"* Too wrapped up in her own thoughts, she could only concentrate on the warmth of Vito next to her and the sultry breeze stirring her thin peasant blouse around her shoulders.

Her throat dried as she braved a glance up into his dark hazel eyes. His gaze probed deep, as if he could see deep inside her to all those soft, suggestible parts she'd buried after Rafe's scam had been revealed.

After her colossal stupidity had been unveiled.

God, she was an idiot for treading down this same terrain with Vito.

Ready to put this farce of a photo behind her, she pulled away from him. "Okay, let's shoot the next location and call it a day."

COULD Christine have killed the mood any faster?

Vito followed her lead as she hustled around the new gardens faster than one of his cars on the final lap. She arranged branches, pruned flowers and deflected all of Giuseppe's sly remarks at full throttle, as if she couldn't wait to put the ordeal of the pictures behind her.

No, truth be told, she acted as though she couldn't wait to put *Vito* behind her.

He puzzled over her sudden retreat while his uncle snapped a few shots at the final location Christine had suggested for his sister's wedding photos. The sun slipped lower on the horizon, casting a faint orange glow on the rose bushes near a small fountain Christine had installed last week. She'd called this little corner her "Ode to Rome" with its classical statue of Venus and the pleasantly weathered marble bench she'd purchased secondhand from his brother Renzo's wife, who worked as an antiques dealer.

Vito had been touched by Christine's thoughtfulness, the tribute to his parents' homeland all the more fitting since she'd salvaged many of the roses from a long-ignored garden of his mother's.

He felt the tension thrumming through her as they stood side by side while Giuseppe snapped their picture. Damn it, why was she in such a hurry to put distance between them? When they'd begun this torturous task, at least they'd both been on the same side—trying to keep from tearing one another's clothes off after all their frustrated efforts to be together.

But something had happened during the course of that first photo, something that made her pull away from him. And damn but he hated thinking he'd disappointed her. Upset her.

Placed in the peculiar position of not having any idea what a woman wanted from him, Vito wasn't sure what to say to make up lost ground. Knowing they'd be finished with the test photos soon, he settled for speaking from the heart while his uncle adjusted the camera settings.

"It means a lot to me that you incorporated my mother's rose garden into the new landscaping." Vito watched her weave a young vine into some wrought-iron trelliswork framing one side of the garden. "Thank you."

A little of the tension seemed to slide out of her shoulders.

"It was my pleasure. People tend to think roses must be fussy flowers because they're so delicate and pretty, but they're actually very hearty." She tilted a peach-colored bloom toward her nose and leaned to inhale its fragrance before meeting his gaze. "They're much tougher than they look."

"That goes double for a certain woman I know." He kept his voice low so that Giuseppe wouldn't hear them, but then he noticed his uncle was otherwise engaged in staring at Mary Jo Kowolski who had just come outside to water her lawn.

"I think this picture looks great," Giuseppe said absently, tossing the camera aside as he moved in Mary Jo's direction. "If we're all set here I think I might go...see how your neighbor's van is working."

Christine looked as though she would have followed his lovestruck uncle if she could have. Instead she moved toward the workshed. "Actually, I need to get back to work, too."

"Wait." Vito insinuated himself between her and her stored tools. "No more running and no more hiding. You're avoiding me now as much as you were those first few weeks after I came home and neither of us is going anywhere until you tell me why."

10

CHRISTINE hadn't realized until that moment how much she appreciated the quiet, non-stressful rewards of planting flowers and shrubs.

Standing her ground, she folded her arms and waited for Vito to move. "I'm sorry, but I'd rather not have a confrontation in the middle of your yard with the neighborhood's nicest gossip and your matchmaking uncle a few yards away."

"Who's having a confrontation?" He looked genuinely surprised. "I just want to talk to you."

She gazed over his shoulder at her tools and the cluster of thatch palms that needed trimming. Work held all the more appeal when the alternative was facing questions she didn't want to answer.

"If you want your sister's wedding to be beautiful, I really should be spending more time on the property." She didn't dare look him in the eye, however, since she'd much rather spend her last ten days here sprawled in bed with Vito and not thinking or talking. Just feeling.

The sun slanted its last purple rays over the backyard while she waited for him to move.

"Then how can I help you?" Vito moved toward the workshed where her tools waited. "You can explain it all to me while we work."

Oh, no, she couldn't. She wouldn't be able to get anything done with him so close to her. He turned her on just *breathing*. She'd never survive seeing all those lean muscles of his in action.

"I don't think that's such a good idea."

"It's a great idea." He dragged her closer to the workshop. "Just give me a tool and point out a project while you clue me into what's going on between us because I'm missing some big part of the picture that you haven't shared."

She reached into the storage area and pulled out a pair of pruning shears and a rake. "I'm sure we both haven't shared a lot of things, Vito. Wasn't that part of the reason for a fling? Keep things simple and easy?"

Although she had to admit that nothing about their summer affair had been simple or easy right from the start and her taking a week to make up her mind. Even the sex that was so good it was transporting couldn't truly be called "simple" since it had complicated her job and compromised her heart.

Vito wanted different things from life than she did. She had no desire to travel the globe and party at an international level. And she'd take her crappy pickup truck over his spit-shined Ferrari any day of the week. Bottom line, she didn't want any part of his lifestyle any more than he seemed inclined to play in the dirt.

"Damn it, Christine, that doesn't mean I want you to make it so simple for me that you don't share things that are bothering you." He took the shears from her and then closed the door to the workshop. "We've still got ten days together and I don't want you to spend them being unhappy."

As she led him to the corner of the yard with the thatch palms, she allowed his words to sink in. And while it was no surprise that the wedding would be their last day together, she wondered for the first time what was in store for them after that. How exactly did one say goodbye to a summer lover?

"I'm not unhappy." She pointed to one of the palm trees that needed a final trimming while she began up the lawn in this corner of the yard she hadn't resodded. If she was lucky, maybe he'd get caught up in the job and forget all about the inquisition.

"Fine, you're not unhappy." He trimmed a few brown, heavy leaves dangling off the dwarf trees. "How about this, *I'm* unhappy knowing that you're holding back whenever we're together and I'm disappointed you don't think you can confide in me."

Was she that transparent, or was Vito Cesare just a damn insightful guy for a superstud race-car driver with houses on two continents? Probably a little of both, she conceded, knowing she couldn't write off Vito as a jet-setting playboy anymore since he'd proved to be so down-to-earth and just plain nice with her.

And how could she blame him for not wanting to

commit to anyone when she'd just recently made that same vow in her own life—much to the disappointment of her inner romantic?

As she raked and thought and pretended not to steal covert glances at Vito's spectacular muscles in action, she figured as long as he'd cornered her, she might as well put her cards on the table. She always appreciated honesty in other people. She could at least be honest with him in return.

When she stopped raking, she realized he'd quit pruning. He stood watching her. Waiting.

"You're right." Standing the rake upright beside her, she gripped the wooden handle for support. Courage. "I am holding back. I can't help that and I'm not going to change that, but I can at least tell you *why*."

Maybe.

Assuming she didn't chicken out and sprint for her pickup truck first.

Vito studied her, his impressive shoulders planted directly between her and her only possible escape vehicle.

Sighing she stuck with her good intentions. "Did you ever have one of those relationships that really screws up your whole life or kind of breaks your heart?"

"Honestly?" He took a step closer, laying the pruning tool on the ground. "I've never really let anybody close enough to do a number on me."

Comforting to know she'd tell her story to a man who had zero means of comparison. Would it have killed him to just nod yes? She tried to remember how much she appreciated his honesty before forging ahead.

"Well, my nightmare dating experience spooked me big-time since I accidentally got engaged to a guy with seven other fiancées."

He blinked. Twice. "Accidentally? How long did you know this guy?"

"Actually, we only met once face-to-face. But we had an online relationship for almost a year before he popped the question in person." And by then she'd been head over heels. Along with a whole slew of other women.

"What an idiot."

"Um. No kidding. But I've learned to forgive myself." Although it hadn't been easy. She'd always set high standards for herself and to fail so miserably and so publicly had been a real blow to her self-esteem.

"Hell, I don't mean you." He reached to stroke his hand over her hair. "I mean that guy must have had a screw loose. No man in his right mind would try to please eight women. Half the guys I know can't even effectively make one woman happy."

She soaked up his touch, thinking that Vito had been really successful in making one woman happy. Her whole body sang with pleasure every time he came within reach.

"The worst part about it was that the news made all the West Coast papers and the story followed me around for months afterward." At least she'd had her work with a landscaping business to keep her busy. She'd found solace in working outdoors with non-judgmental plants. "I've managed to put most of the time out of my mind, but the whole engagement farce really soured me on romance."

And love. And happily-ever-afters. And any man who might be a player.

Frankly, globe-trotting race-car drivers filled the bill. Christine was holding out for a man who appreciated the finer points of home and hearth. Like having something blooming in the garden during every season of the year. And feeling connected to one place.

Hell, Vito Cesare didn't even seem particularly connected to one country.

"I'm not going to pretend that doesn't suck." His hand slid away from her hair before he settled in against one of the thatch palms near the old tire swing. "But you must know it's not fair to write off a whole gender just because one guy was a jack-off."

"I'm not writing off every guy. Only the ones in the twenty-to-forty-year-old demographic. I'm sure the rest of them are just peachy." She shifted away from him, away from the intimacy of sharing a piece of herself. The last thing she needed was Vito feeling sorry for her. Or worse, thinking she had to be the world's most clueless woman.

As she went back to raking—a bit more fiercely than before—she noticed Vito hesitate. When he started to prune the palms again, he worked more slowly than before. No doubt thinking about her dating ineptitude.

"The guy had eight fiancées?"

"If you count me, yes." She shuddered as she unwound an old length of honeysuckle from its stranglehold on an overgrown bush. "Although, I suppose I'd rather not."

"Do you mind if I ask what was so damn appealing about the man that he managed to convince so many women to marry him?"

She looked up at the annoyed tone in his voice. Only then did she realize he'd begun to attack his job with even more ferocity than she'd tackled hers.

The hope that he might feel a smidgen of jealousy died as soon as it began. More likely he was just kicking himself for starting a fling with a wary gardener who wouldn't even spend the whole night in his bed. A man who drove a Ferrari and partied around the world probably wasn't used to such a slow summer.

"Why? You trying to figure out how to make sure I don't lasso you with a cummerbund and drag you down the aisle against your will?"

He tossed the heavy shears aside with little concern for the divot he made in her grass. Technically his grass, but still. Could she help it if she was feeling defensive at all his questions? She hadn't signed on for this when she'd said yes to a summer affair.

"Why the hell would I be worried about you chaining me to your side when you run for a hoe or a spade every time I get within arm's reach of you?" He stole the rake right out of her hand and pitched it next to the pruning shears beneath the swing. "I just want to know what it is this guy did that made you throw all those damn boundaries and gardening tools aside and take a gamble."

Vito stared down into Christine's blue eyes, amazed that he could strip away her landscaping equipment and stand almost toe-to-toe with her, yet she still retained an air of aloof distance. What was it about her that made him want to reach through that gulf between them and haul her over to his side?

The instinct scared him as much as it enticed him.

"He reeled me in with a lot of romantic BS." She hugged her arms around her waist and anchored her fingers in the belt loops of her cargo shorts. "Hearts, flowers and stuff. Poems. Love letters. The hard-core romance things some women still dream about and rarely find in a dating scene that's all about how fast you can score and how often. Obviously I wasn't the only one who fell for the fairy-tale scam."

She held her head high even though a dull flush crawled over her cheeks that couldn't have anything to do with the Florida sun that was almost set by now.

Now he felt like a total heel.

Her moron fiancé had given her the things she really wanted while Vito had given her...what? A good time in the shower? No wonder she wasn't letting him get too close to her.

He wanted to reach for her, to haul her closer and fix this awkwardness somehow, but where would they go from there? What did he really have to offer her once their ten days together were up and he left for Germany? Another year on the racing circuit. Another year living the life he'd put off for so long in deference to his siblings, while Christine had her own business to run.

"You deserve the fairy tale." That much was damn certain. "And not the scam variety. You shouldn't settle for anything less than the real deal."

She gave the tire swing an idle nudge and sent it spinning. "Apparently they call it a fairy tale for a reason. It's not real."

"I know firsthand it's real." Vito stopped the tire, steadying it with his hands before he leaned over one side of it, his elbows perched on the rubber.

"It's a myth, Vito." She slumped over the other half of the tire, her soft scent curling around him as she anchored herself on the opposite side of the frayed rope. "I learned it the hard way, so just let me spare you the trouble of finding out firsthand."

"My brothers and sister all have the fairy tale. My mom and dad did, too." Funny how he hadn't thought about their relationship in a long time. He'd been a teenager when his mother had died in childbirth with his brother Marco and Marco's twin sister who hadn't survived. Perhaps he'd opted not to think about his parents together because for many years afterward, it had been easier *not* to remember. But now, allowing himself to think about his mom and dad as a couple made him smile.

"Maybe it only looked that way on the outside." She turned her head sideways to stare at him across the short space of black rubber, her forehead scrunched with skepticism. "Don't you think some parents sort of fake happiness for the sake of their kids?"

"Not my parents." He peered across the yard to Mrs. Kowolski's house where Uncle Giuseppe was telling her a story that involved both hands and a lot of gesturing. Whatever it was made Mrs. K. laugh. "Mary Jo would vouch for them. Hell, even the most oblivious of neighbors who lived here back then could tell you that the Cesares were crazy in love."

Christine smiled as she propped her head on her elbow to listen. "Really?"

"You know the stereotype about Italians being passionate and expressive?" He stared into Christine's eyes in the falling twilight and wondered how many times his parents had smiled at each other under these same trees. "It didn't matter if my folks were mad, sad or happy—everyone around them knew it. They'd have spats where they'd shout and fling dishes, but when it was over, they were just as obvious about making up. My mother would hang out her bedroom window to blow kisses at my dad when he left for work and he would carry her over mud puddles in the driveway."

"So it was the fairy tale, but it was real at the same time." She ran her finger down the knots in the worn rope tied around the swing. "I don't remember my parents together since my dad left when I was little. I always thought it would be nice to have romance in a relationship but after the whole engagement debacle I guess I'd rather settle for honesty."

"And that's why you decided to have a fling." Understanding finally dawned on him. The various facets of Christine started to fall into place as he realized she had never been a fling kind of girl before. She'd compromised her standards to have a no-strings affair with him because some dirt ball had lied to her so much she no longer believed she could find the happiness she deserved.

"After the rude awakening with Rafe, I thought your idea of no commitment sounded fun. And at least you were being honest with me." She shoved away from the tire, leaving him draped over the top of the swing by himself.

His eyes tracked her as she moved around the yard in the growing dark, her understated curves damn pleasing to the eye as she bent to repair a small divot in the grass.

"What about now?" He shifted off the swing and moved toward her, unable to keep away from her even now that he acknowledged she deserved a hell of a lot more from a relationship than he had to offer. "Has this summer been fun for you?"

Was it selfish of him to want to hear her say yes?

Absolutely.

That didn't stop him from asking the question. And it definitely didn't stop him from following her or sliding his hands around her waist while the night birds started to call and chant around them.

"I like knowing exactly what I'm going to get with you." A smile hitched at her lips as she skimmed her hands up his arms to rest on his shoulders.

"Even if it's a hell of a lot less than you deserve?" He didn't like the idea of her "settling" for anyone. Not even him.

Her eyes focused on his mouth as she arched closer. "Right now, there's only one thing I want from you."

His eyes fell shut as she nipped his lower lip and drew it into her mouth. Wrapping his arms around her tighter, he pressed her body to his, savoring the give of her soft curves along with the flex of trim muscles.

She tasted like the mint leaf she'd given him to try in between Uncle Giuseppe's pictures. And the light floral scent wafting his way could have been her perfume or her flowers. She was as all natural as the name of her landscaping business—a walking advertisement for the benefits of clean, healthy living.

He wanted to inhale her like a breath of fresh air. Take her deep inside him and hold her there.

He'd never met a woman who made him question his path for a moment, but Christine Chandler and her hidden romantic streak made him think about what he'd want from life after racing.

If he ever quit racing, that is.

And as she tugged him toward the house with her slender arms and the powerful lure of her kiss, Vito acknowledged that what he wanted one day in some misty, far-off future was a woman just like this. A woman who wasn't afraid to be romantic and passionate and honest with her feelings.

And maybe he'd never understood what he wanted because he'd never met anyone who harbored all those things inside. And although he wasn't ready to quit racing yet—hell, even if he was, he didn't have a clue what else he'd do for a living—kissing Christine made him realize he wanted this forever someday.

Feet following hers toward the back door, he kept her locked against him all the way across the darkened yard now that night had fallen and Mrs. K. had disappeared inside her house with his uncle. Fingers already straying beneath the hem of her shirt, he traced a path up along the curve of her waist. Her breath hitched as she caught his shoulders, squeezed him more tightly to her.

He wasn't wasting another minute of having her alone and he'd be damned if he'd waste another second of this incredible summer. And who knows? Since she didn't want men in her five-year plan anyhow, maybe she'd still be around Miami by the time he figured out what to do after his racing career.

Although right now he could only seem to think about getting her inside the house. In his bed. And very naked.

Heat streamed through his veins at the feel of her hips swaying against his as she walked. Ready for more, he reached for the door to the house.

Just as the glare from a pair of headlights flashed across their bodies.

"What the hell?" Against his will, Vito broke their kiss and squinted into the light as a car pulled into their driveway.

"Maybe it's someone turning around," Christine offered, her arms still wrapped around his neck, her heart hammering his chest almost as much as his own.

He wanted her to be right, prayed she was right. Too bad the driver cut the engine and the lights at that moment.

Vito swallowed a curse as the car door slammed and a sunny feminine voice echoed across the lawn.

"Call me crazy, but I decided to trek halfway around the world to see this landscaping job for myself." The figure of his sister became visible as she made her way up the drive. "Better cue up 'Here Comes the Bride,' big brother. I'm home!"

11

IT WAS IMPOSSIBLE not to like Giselle Cesare, Christine finally admitted to herself four days later as she finished watering the new annuals she'd planted around the old oak bearing the tire swing.

"We've got to leave in ten minutes to get ready for the bachelorette party, Christine," Giselle shouted to her out the kitchen window, her throaty voice carrying over the soft sprinkle of water all around Christine. "And bachelorettes aren't allowed to have any dirt under their nails."

Christine nodded and smiled and continued to water the flowers, knowing damn well that by the time she went with Vito's sister and her friends to the myriad of salon and spa appointments they had planned today, there was no way she'd have a speck of dirt on her bod.

In the course of the four days Giselle had been back, the fiery Italian chef had moved back into her childhood home in the room between Christine and Vito, effectively halting any chance for covert liaisons with Vito. Because Giselle's fiancé needed to stay overseas for a few more days, Vito's sister had wanted to stay in the house instead of the hotel she owned.

Made total sense, even if it did stall Christine's fling in its tracks.

But as if that hadn't been bad enough, Giselle had commandeered Christine to help her shop for a trousseau, to visit Mrs. K. and review the plans for a wedding cake, to visit the church where the ceremony would take place and to help plan the bachelorette party with a few other girlfriends. But if Christine had been startled at being swept up into bridal plans when she barely knew the bride, Giselle had quickly amended that by appointing herself Christine's new best friend the moment she arrived and broke up the kiss Christine still replayed in her head on a daily—okay, hourly—basis.

Shutting down the sprinkler system, she now headed inside to shower before the spa day preceding the bachelorette party. Coordinated in conjunction with the bachelor party, tonight's event was scheduled to take place at the exotic resort Giselle owned along with a handful of business partners. The idea was that the partying bachelorettes would be able occasionally to check in on the partying bachelors next door. Giselle had hinted there might be some pairing off for a few sexy games she had in mind, but Christine had been too careful about her relationship with Vito to express any more than passing interest in this facet of the night.

Although Giselle had seemed more than willing to talk about her brother, Christine remained determined not to pump her new friend for information about him.

She was only having a fling after all, and she would do well to remember her commitment to being a footloose bachelorette. Besides, the more she knew about Vito, the more she liked him. No need to tread on dangerous terrain.

Still, considering she'd seen little of Vito for over a week now since the out-of-town company started arriving, she had to admit she was looking forward to any game that would put her within liplock range of Vito Cesare.

Maybe at a resort renowned for its sensual atmosphere they would have better luck finding places to tryst than they'd had here.

"Are you ready?" Giselle called into her room just as Christine finished dressing in a T-shirt and shorts.

"All set." She grabbed her bag with her dress for the party tonight, a sexy-as-hell midnight-blue number that she'd picked up on impulse while on one of Giselle's mandatory shopping outings this week.

"My brother's going to totally lose his mind when he sees you in that dress." Giselle moved through the house jingling the keys to her rental car and picking up stray bags on the way as she tugged a small suitcase on wheels behind her. Since her fiancé was due back in town tonight for the party, Giselle would be spending the night with him at Club Paradise and had generously offered rooms to her guests, as well.

"You think?" Christine pulled open the front door for her and stole a big pink pastry box out of Giselle's arms.

Whatever was inside smelled like ginger and vanilla and made her mouth water. "I half wonder if he's already left for Europe in his mind since he's hardly ever here lately."

Shoot. Had she said that? A brainless comment for a woman vowing to keep her relationship light and easy. But Vito seemed to have made himself scarce since Giselle had returned. Even when he was in the house he seemed glued to his computer or entrenched in phone calls conducted in another language.

Not only had she realized that he spoke several tongues fluently in the past few days, she had also learned he had plenty going on in his life besides her. The knowledge stung more than she would ever admit, but it strengthened her resolve not to swoon at his feet when she saw him in a tuxedo at the front of a church in a few days' time.

This man would never be content to remain in Miami forever.

"Not a chance. He's only avoiding you because I'm around. For some ridiculous reason, my brothers still think that because I'm their innocent baby sister, I shouldn't ever be aware of their raging libidos." She rolled her eyes as she unlocked the trunk of the sporty convertible. "As if. I don't think they realize that trying not to think about sex only makes you think about it more."

Grateful for the excuse of loading their gear into the car, Christine tried to think of an appropriate comeback to haul ass out of this conversation. Obviously Giselle was fishing for information about their relationship. Either that or she was trying to give the green light for Christine and Vito to do whatever the hell they wanted to in the house.

Either way, Christine couldn't staunch a twinge of envy for this woman who seemed to have found love and romance along with great sex in her journalist husband Hugh Duncan. Christine had always dreamed about the love and romance part, but after knowing Vito, she couldn't imagine falling in love without the great sex element in place, too.

For that matter, she couldn't even fathom hot and heavy relations with anyone but Vito Cesare. A matter sure to cause an impediment to any future relationships.

"Cat got your tongue on that note, didn't it?" Giselle giggled as she slammed the truck closed and unlocked the car. "Sorry about that. Have you discovered yet that members of my family are apt to say whatever happens to be on their minds? Although I guess Vito is probably the most diplomatic of any of us."

They slid into the car and Christine thought there were worse traits in the world than speaking your mind. Like hiding the truth, for instance. Vito might not be a candidate for love and romance because of his far-flung racing commitments and his unwillingness to let anyone get too close, but at least he would be straight with her.

"I've always appreciated people who are straightforward." Staring out at the occasional glimpses of the Atlantic on their drive toward South Beach, Christine knew she was going to miss Vito and all his exuberant, outspoken relatives when she was finished with this job. In her quest to be independent from her own family, she'd unwittingly pushed her brothers away ever since she'd struck out on her own to go to school in California. Not until now did she realize how much she missed the camaraderie of family. People to watch your back. "That goes for you and your brother both."

"He belongs here, you know." Giselle tapped the steering wheel with a bare fingernail as she pulled onto a causeway toward the beach. "And I know that's unsolicited information, but I feel compelled to point it out to you in case it isn't obvious. I saw him at a couple of his races earlier this summer and he didn't seem up for partying afterward at any of the glitzy events they hold for the drivers. I think he's already squeezed all the fun he's going to out of that career."

Christine cursed her heart for picking up speed at that particular insight. Why should she care?

Of course, her ever-helpful romantic wishful thinking was quick to pipe up that maybe if he would be willing to settle in Miami again, they could follow this fling and see if it led to something real, something far more satisfying...

"He's told me he loves his career." Hadn't he? Or maybe she just guessed as much by the way he treated his Ferrari like an adored offspring. "And while I understand your family's efforts to persuade him to settle down, I can assure you, he has no desire to do anything like that with *me*."

So there.

The smart and streetwise angel on one shoulder stuck her tongue out at the scheming romantic devil perpetually perched on her other one.

"Are you sure about that?" Giselle switched off the car in front of a valet dressed in khakis and a T-shirt proclaiming Club Paradise on the pocket. Turning to stare at Christine while the valet awaited her keys, Giselle gave her a level look. "Because I can tell you right now the consensus of three generations of romantic-minded Cesares and Donzinettis is that Vito is crazy about you whether he kisses you in front of us or not. So please don't hold back on our account, Christine, because we're all rooting for you."

Surprise glued her to her seat for a long moment after Giselle made her transaction with the valet. They were rooting for her? This big, ever-growing group of endless friends and relatives?

The notion would have made her smile if she hadn't been overwhelmed by that level of expectation. What if she didn't want Vito in her life forever?

Liar. Liar. Liar.

She couldn't deny that part of her already did.

As she slid out of the car at the resort, Christine

moved to help Giselle carry in the bags the valet pulled out of the trunk.

Giselle winked at her as she handed Christine the pink box containing some hidden delicious treat.

"If, on the other hand, you're out to break my brother's heart—" She paused for a moment, perhaps waiting for Christine to conjure the worse retribution possible on her own. "We'd all be really disappointed."

Far from being put off by the word of warning, Christine couldn't help but think she never would have let Rafe pull the wool over her eyes if she'd had a sister like Giselle.

Vito was damn lucky to have a family like this.

It was a shame Christine wouldn't be making the big play for him that they wanted. She would respect his wishes and let him go when the time came.

But for tonight, he wouldn't be able to escape her in the man-magnet dress she'd bought for the occasion.

"I can't tell you what the future will bring, Giselle." Christine hurried to keep pace with Vito's sister as she plowed through the doors to Club Paradise. "But I can tell you that for tonight at least, he's all mine."

VITO HAD BEEN to a few bachelor parties in his time, but he didn't think any of his prior groom send-offs had focused so completely on sex.

Head in his hands, he slumped over a cocktail table in the corner of the Moulin Rouge lounge where the bachelor and bachelorette parties were simultaneously taking place. The bar inside Club Paradise was closed to the public tonight, but since Giselle co-owned the resort with three other women, who were all in attendance, she'd been able to reserve the place exclusively for the rowdy crew of bachelors and bachelorettes. Their parties divided only by freestanding Chinese silk screens down the middle of the bar, and Vito caught plenty of glimpses of Christine having a good time with his sister's friends and family on other side of the partitions.

And of course, Giselle's friends had purposely baited the men with their antics to encourage plenty of heads peeking around the dividers. First they'd hosted an informal lingerie party and paraded around their side of the club in naughty negligées.

Then there'd been the noisy striptease lesson given to all the females by a South Beach pro. When Vito had leaned over the screen to complain about the lack of appropriateness of strip lessons at a party where two of his eighty-year-old great-aunts were in attendance, he'd discovered Aunt Livia and Aunt Rosella engaged in full-on rump-shaking beside their stripper teacher.

The sight had sent him back to his own party, determined to hold his peace. But not before he'd spied Christine clutching a slick silver dance pole and practicing her high kicks.

Who the hell could party with the guys when he had a vision of Christine's sleek thigh bared by a generous slit in her midnight-blue dress burned in the back of his retinas?

"Come on, Vito." His brother Nico nudged him in the arm as the rest of the guys let out a loud whoop of appreciation for something in the front of the room. "You're gonna miss the best part if you don't snap out of it."

"Is it just me, or is this completely twisted to be right next to our baby sister talking about sex with all her friends?" Vito grumbled as he rose to join everyone else. "What happened to bachelor parties where all the guys got hammered in some crappy dive bar and threw darts until the designated driver carted everyone home?"

Not that getting hammered sounded particularly fun either, but at least then he wouldn't be stuck listening for hints of Christine's voice in the swirl of raucous chatter on the other side of the silk screens. Or straining his eyes for another glimpse of her through a gap in the partition he just happened to sit near.

"Since when do you like playing darts?" Nico did a double take as he noticed the partition gap. Lingering near the screen, he stared through the wall toward Giselle's party. "Remember that Christmas when Marco was thirteen and he wanted a darts set? You lectured him for two months on the dangers of darts and then— *Hello, beautiful.*"

Vito blinked, knowing damn well the brother closest to his own age wasn't talking to him anymore. "What?"

"I'm checking out my fiancée." Nico's eyes never swerved from their target. Apparently he'd gotten an

eyeful of his power executive future wife, Lainie Reynolds. "I was hoping she'd let her hair down tonight and
have fun, and there she is, chugging down a martini
like it was soda pop." He spied for another moment before straightening. "She usually works too damn hard.
It's good for her to have fun."

"I'm sure you'll be a positive influence in that arena."
Vito grinned, thinking about how Nico had managed to
devote his whole life to playing games. First as an NHL
goalie with the Florida Panthers and now as a hockey
coach who also ran training camps for peewee players.
"Have you taken her skating yet?"

"She hates the helmet I make her wear, but she's got
real aptitude. Not to mention killer instincts. She can
cross-check with the best of them."

Vito's gaze darted back to the partition again, wondering where Christine had gone. "You're lucky you
found someone to put up with you, bro. I'm happy for
you."

"I highly recommend hooking up on a permanent basis. Dating is for suckers." Nico dragged him toward
the front of the bar where the guys were all gathered
around a table and a few people were—taking the partitions down?

His night was beginning to look up. Maybe he could
find Christine and kidnap her from the party. Steal a
few minutes alone somewhere in this huge resort. Or
better yet, cart her back to his room for the night. The
best part of having this shindig at Club Paradise had

been that partygoers were all encouraged to spend the night, courtesy of their hostess.

"I never imagined you'd be the poster boy for long-term commitment after all the years you fielded screaming groupies in the NHL." As one of Giselle's friends carried a big pink pastry box over to the bar, Vito had to admire how far his brother had come.

"And I never imagined you wouldn't be the commitment king after all those years you spent raising a family." Nico kept his eye trained on the pastry box, already changing directions to follow the promise of food. "You were so damn good at the lectures and advice that went along with the patriarch role, we all kind of thought you liked it."

He *had* liked it, damn it. He just hadn't been ready for the job at the time.

And now?

Now he was the second-ranked Formula One driver in the world. An accomplishment he took great pride in. Even if it had slowly overtaken some areas of his life he used to enjoy.

"I did," he admitted, but by now Nico was making a beeline for the bar and the pink box everyone seemed to be gathering around.

What now?

Spying Christine sandwiched between the stripper tutor, and his new sister-in-law, Esmerelda Giles, Vito tried to catch her eye to see if she'd be interested in blowing off the rest of the party.

Too bad her eyes were glued on the damn box along with everyone else's.

"What gives?" He hustled to keep up with Nico weaving through the crowd.

"I opened one of Giselle's pink pastry boxes before and got the surprise of my life," Nico shot back darkly, his brow furrowed as he glared at Giselle climbing onto the bar to address the group.

Curious, Vito stuck around long enough to hear what his sister had to say even though he had every intention of making off with Christine at the first possible opportunity. Already his feet sidled in her direction since he was determined to stop thinking about sex and start acting on the impulse.

"And now for my favorite party game," Giselle was saying between the kisses she blew at her fiancé, Hugh. She lifted up the box and opened it with a flourish. "I've made a batch of my famous Kama Sutra cookies and I invite you all to indulge."

There were squeals of surprise and a general rush of excitement through the guests as they got a look at whatever the hell Kama Sutra cookies might be. Vito noticed Nico and Renzo both clapping hands over their eyes.

Not a good sign.

He had almost reached Christine's side, however, and right now he was more concerned about getting his hands on her in that incredible dress she wore than worrying about whatever mayhem his sister had in mind.

All around him, guests were scrambling for the cookies. Including Christine.

Vito took advantage of all the people in motion, easily sliding alongside the stripper to insinuate himself into position next to Christine. His thigh brushed hers as he maneuvered closer, the contact delectable but all too brief.

"Hi." She smiled at him, her lips slick with shiny pink lip gloss that begged to be licked off.

He would have propositioned her then and there if Giselle hadn't whistled for attention again.

"Now that everyone has a cookie, you all need to find a partner and form boy-girl teams," his sister continued, a wicked smile on her face as she winked at Hugh. "The object of the game is to see who can copy their Kama Sutra position most effectively without taking off their clothes. Ready? Go!"

Vito hoped to hell the game wasn't as racy as it sounded. Since when was his little sister familiar with the damn Kama Sutra?

And aside from that unsettling thought, Vito didn't stand a chance of recreating any sexy position with Christine without ripping his clothes off in all due haste. He was toast for this game.

"Well, partner?" Christine peered around the room slowly, as if to be sure they were paired up together for the game. Sure enough, everyone else from Aunt Rosella to the exotic dancer had already claimed their partner. "Are you ready to play?"

A challenge twinkled in her blue eyes, her chin tilted high as she stared up at him. He knew if he lowered his gaze he'd find the soft enticement of her half-covered breasts squeezed into a stretchy knit dress with wide-set spaghetti straps. Of course, he didn't dare look down or he'd follow his gaze with his lips and kiss every square inch of the creamy skin her outfit exposed.

"Not in public." He couldn't afford to so much as lay a finger on her after so many days away from her. "I need to see you alone."

She shook her head slowly as she looked down at her cookie, her regret obvious in her voice. "It's too bad you don't want to play, Vito. We sure had a humdinger of a position to act out."

Handing him the sweet, Christine turned on one towering high heel and walked away. Leaving him with only a sugary treat for comfort.

Looking down at the airy confection in his palm, Vito distinguished the words "Queen of Heaven" written in tiny frosting letters. But the workmanship in the words was nothing compared to the artistic rendition of a naked couple entwined in the most intimate of positions. While a woman lay on her side, her long red hair spread on the bed behind her, a man straddled her bottom leg and clenched her upper leg in his hands. He entered her from this sideways position, cradling her thigh to his chest while he...

Holy hell.

Vito ignored the molten lava suddenly running through his veins at the heady appeal of the image. Because suddenly, all he could think about was the fact that Christine had implied she wanted to do this with him.

Now.

Taking his cookie with him, Vito couldn't sprint out of the party fast enough.

12

HER PULSE thrummed as footsteps sounded behind her.

Christine clicked her way down the coral-colored marble corridor inside Club Paradise, the music of the Moulin Rouge lounge fading as she moved deeper into the hotel. Were those Vito's footsteps, or someone else's?

A few guests of the resort walked by her, a man dressed in a sleek suit with clinging, half-clad women on either side of him. An intriguing arrangement, but not to her personal taste. When it came to Vito Cesare, she had no interest in sharing.

The footsteps behind her sounded closer, sending a shiver over her skin. A delicious sixth sense made her body hum with anticipated pleasure and told her exactly who approached.

"Wait." Strong arms slid around her from behind, halting her in her tracks underneath a mammoth chandelier.

She caught his scent and closed her eyes as he pressed her back against him.

"I thought you didn't want to play." Her head fell

back to rest on his shoulder for just a moment, exposing her neck in case he happened to lean closer. To kiss her.

She hadn't realized how much suppressed desire had been building inside her the past few days, but now that she had Vito's hands on her again, she all but combusted in the middle of the elegant Club Paradise corridor.

"I said not in public." He leaned over her to touch the wall in front of her.

To press an elevator button, she realized as she pried her eyes open.

"Does that mean you'd be willing to seek out a more private arrangement?" She turned in his arms, visions of the Kama Sutra cookie still dancing in her head.

The elevator door slid open and he tugged her inside, the heat of his hand enveloping hers.

"That means you don't have a prayer of spending another second at my sister's bachelorette party." He stabbed the button for the second floor with one finger while the doors swished closed. "So I hope you didn't have any plans for more lingerie purchasing or striptease lessons tonight."

One hand still braced on the elevator wall, he stared down at her with hazel eyes turned so brown almost all traces of green had fled. He didn't touch her anywhere, yet she could already anticipate his hands on her everywhere, her whole body vibrating with sensual hunger.

"Maybe it's time to put the striptease lessons into practice." She'd never ventured into those kinds of bedroom adventures with other guys, but something about Vito made her feel very uninhibited. Daring.

The elevator arrived on the second floor, the car settling to a stop before the doors rolled open again. As she stepped out into the plush Persian carpet of the hallway, it occurred to her she had no clue where they were headed. His room, maybe?

Sure enough, he already had a keycard in hand as he guided her to the right down the hallway.

"As much as I would love to see that any other time, tonight I don't think I can wait another second." He paused in front of a door labeled Xanadu and inserted his key. "Do you know how many days it's been since I've had you all to myself?"

Too many.

Still, her heart rate did a little skip-jump at the thought of him wanting her all this time. Her thighs quivered at the implication that he wasn't going to wait anymore.

Her throat went dry, her scattered thoughts too jumbled and sex-starved to figure out how long it had been since they'd been able to get naughty in Vito's bed. Or in the shower. Or on the dining room table.

Following him inside, she blinked at the quick flash of bright lights before he turned down the dimmer switch.

"This is Xanadu?" Her gaze ran around the walls painted creamy white with hints of gold showing through. Lights suspended from gilt chains hung around the room, their amber glass globes reflecting the gold and making the whole room shimmer. Eastern-inspired furnishings in bright jewel-tone fabrics crowded around a fireplace that had leapt to life as soon as Vito switched on the lights.

"I think it's based on the Coleridge poem, something about 'In Xanadu did Kubla Khan a stately pleasure dome decree...'" He gestured toward a closed door off to one side of the living area. "Or at least that's what I guessed after I saw the poem framed above the bed."

Bed.

The word had never sounded so erotic as it did coming from Vito's lips.

Her mind had already sprinted into the bedroom, envisioning all the things they could do to one another—for one another—before the night was through. Or at least before she went back to her room. Because no matter how much her body craved Vito's tonight, she couldn't tease her heart by waking up with him tomorrow morning.

Whatever connection they had formed over the course of the summer, it would end after Giselle's wedding. Six days and counting.

Which meant they'd better make every moment count tonight.

WHAT WAS she thinking?

Vito never thought he'd see the day where he'd be standing in the middle of an exotic hotel room with a woman who oozed sensuality the way Christine did and end up agonizing over what she was thinking, yet he found himself doing just that. She'd been too quiet since they'd entered the room, making him wonder if she had second thoughts.

He placed the Kama Sutra cookie he'd carried up from the bachelor party on a decorative end table.

"What's on your mind, Christine?" He reached for her hand, savoring the soft slide of her cool fingers over his skin. She'd painted her nails today—pale, shimmering pink. No rings adorned her fingers, no rocks or decorations for an all-natural beauty. Her sunny smile and lightly tanned skin would make the perfectly made-up and surgically enhanced groupies at the Grand Prix look as though they were trying way too hard.

Her gaze tracked to the cookie he'd set aside.

"Just wondering if you're so confident in your bedroom abilities that you don't even need to look at a diagram." The teasing note in her voice reassured him she wasn't having doubts. Or if she had been worried about anything before, she wasn't anymore.

"It's not that I'm overconfident." He slid her tiny silver purse from her fingers and laid it on the arm of a chair. Pulling her deeper into the room, he admired the way the golden light from the hanging fixtures highlighted the myriad shades of brown in her hair. "It's just that I happen to have a certain level of familiarity with the Kama Sutra."

Pausing when they reached the bare expanse of floor

in front of the fireplace, he lifted a hand to the shoulder strap of her blue dress and traced the strap over her shoulder to the end of her collarbone and down to the soft skin above her breast. Backtracking his trail, he skimmed back up the skin underneath the strap, and then eased his way down again until he flicked the strap off her shoulder altogether.

A delicate shiver swayed her whole body.

"You wicked, wicked man." Her breathless tone didn't convey the same censure as her words. If anything, she made wickedness sound like high praise. "Is that because you read Eastern sex texts just for fun? Or have you been learning your material firsthand from your scads of women strewn across the globe?"

Leaning closer to the shoulder he'd bared, Vito licked a line where the strap had been and then gently blew on the places his tongue had touched. His reward was another shiver and Christine's eyes falling to half mast.

"Forget I asked," she murmured, her hands reaching to tangle in his hair. "However you learned your skills, Cesare, you've got a good game."

"It's mostly book knowledge." He answered her question anyway, nudging her other strap off her shoulder. "Some guys watch low-budget porno in between girlfriends to keep them entertained. I read."

"Are you telling me I'm having my first fling with a sex scholar?" She opened her eyes to peer at him through her long lashes. "You're going to be a very tough act to follow."

He didn't want to think about anyone following him. Couldn't stand the idea of anyone else ever touching her this way.

"Maybe I want to make myself irreplaceable." Fingers roving down the back of her knit dress found the zipper and inched the tab down. "Unforgettable." Without the straps to keep it in place, her dress drifted downward along with the zipper, revealing hints of sexy black satin and creamy skin. "Or maybe I feel the need to erase all memory of your fiancé from your mind."

She smiled as the stretchy blue fabric landed around her ankles, leaving her clad in an outfit that looked as though it could have been borrowed from the stripper downstairs. Stepping from the pile of dark material, she landed right in his arms.

"That would be a very good thing." Her fingers walked up his tie to loosen the knot and slide it off his neck. "Do you have any fancy Eastern love tricks in mind to make me forget anyone else I've ever been with?"

He stared at the black satin bustier with lace insets and a bright blue ribbon tying it together. The matching black bikini bottoms echoed the theme with a blue bow situated just below her navel.

"It's going to take a hell of a trick to make tonight as memorable for you as this outfit has been for me." He couldn't remember ever seeing anything so damn appealing. The only things missing were the leather work boots that made him crazy for her. "You look incredible."

She toyed with the ends of the ribbon between her breasts. "Giselle said no one could leave her party without appropriate bachelorette garb."

He slid the silky ribbon out of her fingers to savor it with his own. "Then I guess I owe the bride a big thank you."

Then again, Christine could have showed up tonight in jeans and a T-shirt and he would have salivated himself dry.

"What about you, Cesare? Do you have any surprises for me underneath your clothes?" Her hands moved over his buttons, unfastening them in a swift, easy rhythm.

"What I have for you shouldn't come as any surprise." He seized her shoulders as she tugged his shirt from his pants.

"That doesn't make it any less welcome." She splayed her hand across the front of his trousers. Drew one finger up the hard length of him.

He reached for his belt buckle while his eyes crossed. Unfastening the leather, he slid her hand away while he shed his pants and tossed them over a couch near the fireplace.

"I'm going to need that damn cookie diagram after all if you keep that up. I can't even remember my own name when you touch me like that."

"Looks like I have a few tricks of my own, doesn't

it?" She stalked closer with her toned legs and killer lingerie, backing him against a coffee table pulled close to the fireplace.

"You're definitely well-armed." And he loved watching her put all those sexy attributes to use after the long weeks she'd kept them hidden under her work clothes.

"But I don't think we need to use the diagram."

"We don't?"

"I've got our position memorized." Smiling, she reached behind him and plucked a dark quilt from the couch. With a snap of her wrist she spread the blanket on the floor behind them, right in front of the decorative fireplace that contributed minimal heat to the room. "Come with me and I'll show you."

He followed her down to the floor, cradling her head in his hand until she settled herself on the blanket. His body stretched on top of hers, he couldn't believe how long it had been since he'd touched her this way.

How the hell could he ever go that long without touching her again?

Shutting down thoughts that only frustrated him, he concentrated on the here and now. Her.

Because right now, he couldn't think of anything that mattered more to him.

"Vito?"

Christine started to panic when she saw that look in his eyes again. More than a "do-me baby" glance, Vito's dark gaze hinted at deeper emotions. The kind that thrilled and terrified her. The kind that threatened to break her heart all over again if she wasn't careful.

"Yeah?" His hands surveyed her whole body, testing every curve and hollow while he watched her with dark eyes.

She couldn't allow herself to get drawn in by those gorgeous eyes of his. Didn't dare to let her romantic heart go aflutter just because he was willing to take all the time in the world to make her feel better than she'd ever felt before.

Concentrate on the heat. The chemistry. The way Vito's body felt stretched out over hers.

She tugged at the layer of lace that covered her, the only remaining barrier between them. "Will you help me out of this?"

Levering himself up on his hands, he inched downward until his mouth was level with her breasts. Poised above her in a shallow push-up, he bent his teeth to her ribbon and gave it a tug.

"I'll take that as a yes." She sighed with pleasure as his warm breath fanned gently over the tops of her breasts. Her fingers moved to his biceps flexed so enticingly above her. She smoothed her way over the hard ridges of muscle, admiring the sleek definition of each one as the firelight played over his bronze skin.

But then Vito was pulling the rest of her bustier ribbon loose, and her thoughts scattered like seeds in the wind. His tongue flicked down the valley between her breasts before claiming one aching nipple.

She arched up against him, urging him closer while the rest of her black lace bustier slid away. Her thighs twitched beneath him, ready for more. If she could only focus on the next orgasm, on having him deep inside of her, then maybe she'd forget about all his soft touches and gentle caresses, the way he cared how she felt instead of thinking about what he wanted.

"Make love to me." She whispered the words, but there was a note of command in her tone he couldn't mistake. She needed him now. "Show me this 'Queen of Heaven' position."

"Soon." He savored her breast like a connoisseur at a feast. Slow. Appreciative.

It was enough to make her knees weak. Her heart melt.

"But I want to try more positions after that one," she blurted, desperate to distract from those exquisite touches so she could simply lose herself in the hard, heated rhythm of hungry sex. "You can teach me."

His lips broke away from one swollen breast. He eased his hand down her belly to stray over her damp satin panties. "There's more to the Kama Sutra than sex positions."

Her breath caught in her throat as he eased aside the elastic on one leg to skim a finger over her slick heat. "Really?"

Her voice came out as little more than a squeak.

"There's a whole section on kissing we ought to try sometime." He twisted his finger into the waistband of her panties and dragged them down her thighs until she was as naked as him.

Blood pulsed through her so hard she was aware of every heartbeat between her thighs. He bent to rub his cheek along her thigh, the bristly hair around his chin lightly scratching her. "You want me to show you some of them?"

The muscles all around her belly tightened. Heat knifed through her to the spot he touched, his lips so close...

"I don't know if..." She trailed off, unable to speak once he dipped a kiss to her thigh.

"There's the bowed kiss. The twisted kiss. The satisfied kiss." As he spoke, he moved nearer and nearer to the place that craved his kiss most.

Heat flooded her limbs, coiled inside her as she tensed. She didn't dare move as she watched him hover over her in the firelight.

"Then there's the vibrant kiss that involves just a little bit of vibration..." He leaned forward to demonstrate, his lips grazing the slick center of her moments before she flew apart, his mouth calling forth the most knee-buckling orgasm known to womankind.

Spasms rocked her on and on while he touched her, whispered to her, kissed her with those wicked, knowing, amazing kisses. When the aftershocks finally ceased, she reached for him, needing him deep inside her.

He was already poised above her, condom in place to

protect her in that endlessly thoughtful way she'd learned was part of this man's nature. While she'd panted and sighed in toe-curling fulfillment, he'd been thinking of her, taking care of her in so many little ways she'd never known she wanted.

Thighs falling open for him, she threaded her fingers though his hair, tugged him closer as he eased his way inside.

"I'll never underestimate the power of a kiss again," she confided, wrapping her legs around him as if to hold him there forever. Or at least all night. She couldn't possibly stay with him long enough.

"And we haven't even gotten to the positions yet," he reminded her, untwining her ankles so that he could grip one of her thighs. Lift it.

He turned himself ever so slightly so that he straddled one of her legs and kept the other bent against his chest. The penetration was so thorough, so complete she felt possessed on the most elemental level.

A cry built in her throat as they moved together and she neared that sensual brink again all too soon. Just as she hit the sweetest high of her life right in time with Vito's, she realized why they called this particular position the Queen of Heaven.

As stars twinkled all around her she knew she'd catapulted straight into the stratosphere.

13

LATER THAT NIGHT, Vito lay awake in bed and stroked Christine's hair while she slept. A stray shaft of moonlight trickled in between the curtains of his bedroom, casting a soft blue haze over her features.

Thinking about what they'd shared earlier, he realized his whole world had ground to a halt for the first time since he'd taken up racing.

Ever since he'd left the States almost six years ago, he had been moving through life at light speed trying to make up for lost time. And even though it had been fun for a while, he had to admit that for the last year, everything around him had been a blur, kind of like the way things looked through his car windshield at two hundred miles per hour.

But tonight, everything had stopped.

Something about Christine had called him out of the fast-moving streak his life had become and made him want to sit still. Savor. Enjoy. Maybe that had been part of her appeal all along, he thought now as he watched her tug the sheet more tightly to her in sleep.

This summer was the first time he'd spent more than a week in Miami since he'd left home. And it wasn't just because he needed to get the house ready for Giselle's wedding. He easily could have flown back and forth all summer the way he'd planned to before he met Christine.

His perpetually restless feet hadn't been called to move in six weeks, preferring to stick close to the woman who occupied all his thoughts lately. But tonight, holding her in his arms while she fell asleep, he'd realized that there was more to this attraction than he could possibly explore during one summer.

Because he loved Christine.

Lying back on the bed, he let the revelation slide over him, waiting for the fear to set in. The second thoughts. He had a career abroad, after all. A career he was passionate about.

But as the clock ticked off another hour and the moonlight changed to the first rays of dawn filtering through the curtains, he still wasn't scared. Just excited. And crazy about her. And in love.

Too bad love alone wouldn't help him figure out how to make a long-distance relationship work. Nor would it provide an alternate career for him in Miami so that he could stay with her here.

When his cell phone rang, he scrambled to answer it before it woke Christine. Who the hell would call him at this hour? Unless...

"Yeah?"

"Vito, it's Oswald." The clipped tones of his publicist rolled over the airwaves. "I know you're busy doing the family thing, but I need you here today for some race preliminaries. Do you want to make the arrangements or do you want me to?"

"Damn it, Ozzie. Can't you handle the preliminaries?" He couldn't jet off to Germany today. Christine deserved better than that.

Then again, maybe she'd be upset when she woke up to discover she'd spent the whole night in his bed. A first for the woman who held on to her boundaries even more tightly than she clutched her sheet under her chin. Besides, she hadn't been the one to fall in love overnight. He was the only one slipping off the deep end for her.

"I thought I could manage things, but there is a lot more media interest here than they anticipated. You can come over, do a few days of interviews and still be back in plenty of time for the ceremony."

Obviously Oswald didn't know squat about Italian family weddings. Giselle had ten different events lined up between now and then. Still, maybe she'd forgive him if he could go over there and either figure out how to convince Christine to move abroad with him, or else find a way to walk away from his career.

She stirred beside him, perhaps sensing the tension quickly threading through him.

"I'll be there. But I'll need you to meet me at the airport because I've got a lot to take care of this trip." His future, and with any luck, Christine's rode on it.

SOMETHING was rotten in the state of Denmark. Or in this case, on the other side of the king-size bed in the Xanadu suite.

Christine held her breath as Vito disconnected his call, waiting to find out what had him looking so tense. Worried.

Distant.

Wasn't this why she hadn't allowed herself to spend a whole night with him up until now? She hadn't wanted to face the morning-after awkwardness, hadn't been ready to see Vito's careful way of extricating himself from her arms. Her life.

"I'd better go." She blurted out the words to ensure she said them before he did. Scrambling out of the bed and dragging the sheet with her, she kept reminding herself this was just a fling. No need for her to feel so damn disappointed this morning.

Just a fling. Just a fling. Just a—

"Don't go." He slid an arm around her waist as she dropped her dress over her head. "Stay here. Sleep a little longer."

Concentrating very hard on the effort, she managed to curl her lips into what she hoped was a lighthearted grin. "Sounds like you've got people to see and places to go, and frankly, so do I." At 6:00 a.m. Yeah, right. Her only plan for today had been to attend Giselle's Hangover Brunch at eleven o'clock this morning.

As per Giselle's instructions, Christine had planned on goofing off a certain amount over the next few days before the wedding since her work on the Cesare property was just about finished. She'd come in on time and almost exactly on budget after sweating out every single purchase she'd made. All she needed to do now was keep everything watered and trimmed so it looked lush for the reception.

She waited for Vito to release her, but that warm, muscular arm of his remained around her waist. Tugged her back toward the edge of the bed to sit beside him in the tangle of sheets where he had taught her the pleasure of all his different kisses.

"I do have someplace to go," he admitted, though he did a damn good job of seeming to regret it. "I've got a race after the wedding and I thought I'd be able to skip all the preliminary events, but apparently I need to put in a quick appearance before the weekend."

The stab to her heart was quick. Efficient. Devastating.

Logically, she knew it shouldn't be since he had prepared her for this right along. Of course, last night she'd let go of her last remaining shreds of logic by staying with him all through the night. Making love to him over and over again until it seemed as though they weren't just sharing bodies. They were sharing hearts. Minds.

Somehow, she'd committed the classic error of mistaking physical affection for—dear God—love.

Even as she admitted as much to herself, her romantic heart mourned the fact that Vito would be checking out of her life mere hours after she'd become irrevocably attached to him.

"Sounds fun," she lied, knowing she'd never be the kind of woman who could tag along in some star driver's entourage, pretending to find small talk about engines interesting and faking that she liked caviar.

They lived in two different worlds, even if he made a good show of seeming to fit into hers.

"I meant to tell you about the race before." His dark eyebrows knit together as he scowled. His naked body rippled with muscles in all the right places. "I don't know why I didn't. I guess my whole life over there seems far away when we're together."

She held herself very still, certain if she allowed herself to move, she'd somehow jar loose a tear. And damn it, she couldn't allow that. She'd known the rules going into this and she had no one to blame but herself if she'd gotten hurt anyhow.

"I'll bet it does. I'm sure you don't usually get sucked into pruning palm trees or come home to find birdseed in your kitchen when you're overseas, do you?"

His smile made her heart ache. "That's what made this summer so fun for me."

But...

She could hear the unspoken word hovering, casting a shadow on their time together. He might have had fun, but it was still time to go.

"Nevertheless, the time has come to bail, right?" She sprang to her feet again, unable to bear the temptation of his body so close to hers and unwilling to sit still for any long-winded goodbye without bawling her eyes out. She'd thought it had hurt when Rafe had turned out to be a fraud?

That was a paper cut compared to the gushing open wound Vito's departure would leave behind.

"I'm not bailing, Christine." He rose to his feet, shrugging his way into his clothes while she made a valiant effort to stuff her undergarments into her tiny purse and tried not to notice that heartbreakingly gorgeous body of his. "I'll be back for the wedding and you promised me you'd go with me. Nothing's changed about our date this weekend."

Only because he needed her to run interference for the matchmakers in his family, right? Attending the wedding would be like a stick in the eye for her now that she'd gone and fallen in love against her better judgment.

"If you can't make it back, I'll understand." Maybe it would be better if he just stayed abroad. Skipped the wedding so she didn't have to suffer through all those "I dos" and "I love yous" with him a few feet away.

Oh God, it was going to be awful.

"We both know my sister would kill me if I didn't get back here for the wedding." Fully clothed now, Vito reached for her while she fidgeted with her purse. "And we need to have a long talk once I get back."

"You told me from the start you wanted to keep this simple, Vito. Let's not muck it up now by dragging out the goodbyes." It would be so much easier if they could just fast-forward through the heartbreak. Skip all the parts about wanting to stay friends and having a nice life.

She edged out of the bedroom, closer to the door of the suite.

"This isn't goodbye." He followed her, but didn't keep her from turning the knob. "I mean it, Christine. We're going to the wedding together and we're going to have the time of our lives. You've worked so hard all summer you deserve to enjoy the rewards. Oh and before I forget..."

He reached for an envelope on a table near the door while she fought to remain as calm and unruffled as him.

"Giuseppe wanted me to give you this." He handed her the thick envelope with her name scrawled across the front. "I know he's been too caught up with chasing Mrs. Kowolski to comment much lately, but you've done a great job with the yard. It looks better than ever."

Fingers clutching the heavy white packet, she knew she'd never forget this landscaping project, a job she'd poured her whole heart and soul into. "I thought Giuseppe wanted me to take a check?"

Vito's phone started to ring again, scattering her thoughts. She ought to just take the money and run. Funny how the compensation had been so important to her when she first started.

And while the money still represented the ability to keep her business afloat until she could make All Natural a big success, somehow in the course of the last weeks her business had taken a back seat to her happiness.

"Is cash okay?" Vito tensed, ignoring the ringing phone. He leaned closer as if to kiss her.

Her eyes fluttered but didn't close. She couldn't afford to show him any moment of weakness now. Turning her cheek, she felt the warmth of his lips on her skin, unable to kiss him back when her heart burned with hurt.

"It's fine. Perfect." She pulled the door open the rest of the way and stepped out into the hallway. "I'll see you Saturday at the ceremony, Vito. Have a safe flight."

Tears already stinging her eyes as she walked to the elevator, Christine thought it was a good thing her only destination was a Hangover Brunch this morning.

If her eyes were a little red and swollen, she should blend right in.

It wasn't until hours later that she opened the fat white envelope Vito had given her to discover the bonus money inside. A very fat bonus she knew damn well cost-conscious Giuseppe would have never given her since he'd spent so much time making sure she juggled the project to come within a very strict budget.

Not to mention the fact he'd wanted to pay her with a check.

Which meant *Vito's* bank account had provided all

that cash before he blew out of town. His idea of giving her fledgling business a boost since she was so obviously struggling in her first year? Or was this payment for other services rendered?

Steam rolled out her ears to consider either scenario, her anger a welcome alternative to thinking about the ache in her heart.

Either way, Christine would have a few choice words for him by the time the wedding rolled around.

BY THE TIME Giselle's wedding arrived, Vito had no choice but to admit Christine must be mad at him.

Five days after Christine had walked out of his hotel suite, he sat in the back room of the Coral Gables church he'd attended his whole life, surrounded by his brothers and Giselle's groom, Hugh Duncan. How could he have screwed things up so badly with Christine and not even realized it? He stared out a small window overlooking the parking lot and hoped he'd see her old truck pull in, while behind him Nico tried to get his tie straight and Renzo heckled him about the lack of refinement in hockey players.

Vito only half listened, cursing himself for taking off for the race preliminaries in the first place. He'd called Christine from Germany every day but no one was ever home. Even his sister had been no help since she'd been immersed in her wedding plans and enjoying her time with family and friends around her. She always told him Christine was busy in the one of the gardens or that she'd already left for the day.

Apparently she'd moved out of the Cesare house while he'd been gone, leaving no forwarding address. Now that her job was through, he supposed, she'd moved back to wherever it was she came from.

Too bad he had absolutely no clue where that would be.

As far as he knew, she didn't live in the area. Yet she was starting a business in Miami so she couldn't have gone far. Still, what if he needed to get in touch with her in an emergency? Like now, for instance.

"Hey, Vito," Nico shouted over his impromptu wrestling match with their youngest brother Marco, who was starting his second year at Harvard this fall. "Isn't it the groom who gets the jitters before the ceremony? You're supposed to be calming Hugh down, not getting all the rest of us wired."

"Jitters my ass." Worried, yeah. But not jittery. Yet. "Don't make me have to brawl with you on your sister's wedding day." His gaze never left the parking lot where there was still no sign of Christine's truck.

Nico let out a whoop as he pinned Marco's hand to an old wooden school desk in the small dressing room. Moonwalking a victory dance over to join Vito at the window, he clapped an arm around his brother's shoulder.

"That's why we need you around town again, bro. No one else in the family can offer to kick my ass and actually back it up." He cast a sly look toward their brother Renzo, whom Marco had to sit on to keep from disproving the claim. "Seriously. It's been good to have you around this summer."

"I'm going to stay this time." Vito's quiet announcement turned the whole room slack-jawed for a two-count before all his brothers started talking at once.

"You're going to quit racing?"

"You'd really move back here?"

But Nico nailed it as he stared out the window with him. "This is about her, isn't it?"

"Damn straight." It was all about her.

Christine.

There hadn't been two minutes in the past five days when he hadn't thought about her. He should have realized sooner how important she'd become to him. Should have cleared things up with her about their future before he left.

But he'd been so damn confused about how to make it happen, how to ditch his commitments and make a life for himself here.

"What if she doesn't show today, bro?" Nico asked the same question Vito had been asking himself all morning.

And he gave him the only answer he would allow.

"She has to."

14

SHE HAD at least to put in an appearance.

Christine gave herself a pep talk in a back alley behind the church, unable just to park the truck and go inside. She'd been circling the block for almost ten minutes now, but once she saw the bride's limo pull up to the church she knew she couldn't put this off any longer.

She'd have to face Vito sometime, if only to give him back his money. Although she'd been very nice and patient with Vito's Uncle Giuseppe when they cleared up the whole issue of payment three days ago, she'd been more than a little frustrated by his insistence that Vito was only trying to thank her for the job she'd done on the yard.

Who thanked their landscaper with a tip that could have put a down payment on a new car? If Vito had liked her work, he could have given her a box of chocolates. Or Mary Jo Kowolski's lemon cookies.

But this was the kind of over-the-top, way-too-generous gesture that seemed to suggest he thought she needed a helping hand. As if she couldn't run a profitable business on her own and needed someone to pave her way.

Either that, or he had only given her the extra cash to assuage his guilty conscience. Maybe he gave her money because he would never give her anything so valuable as his heart.

Hating that scenario even more than the first, Christine slammed the door of her truck with a little extra wrist action. Hearing her old truck groan in response, she immediately felt contrite. Considering she wouldn't be using Vito's money for a down payment on a new truck, she had no business treating her worn-out vehicle with anything but the utmost TLC.

She hurried across the tarmac, stepping double-time in an effort to make sure she was seated before the bridesmaids made their entrance. As she skirted around the limo, one sleek, tinted window lowered and a slender arm waved her over to the car.

Smiling in spite of herself as strains of Sinatra's "Summer Wind" drifted from the long, dark luxury vehicle, she peered inside to see the bride surrounded by the three other women who owned a piece of Club Paradise with her, and Renzo's wife the museum director. They looked like the perfect flower arrangement as the bridesmaids' bright fuchsia skirts billowed about their knees and the bride's white lace train took center stage in the middle seat.

Giselle passed her plastic champagne cup to Summer Farnsworth, a kinky-haired blonde with a single fuchsia clip-on braid twining through her platinum curls. Scooching forward, Giselle peered out the car window to be sure the coast was clear before leaning out to talk.

"My brother is going crazy, Christine. Absolutely, nutzoid, call-the-house every two hours crazy to find out if I've heard from you." She fidgeted with an orange blossom in her hair. "I know I can't tell you what to do when it comes to your love life, but I can tell you this." She pointed her finger in Christine's face, her French manicure as perfect as the rest of her. "Don't you break his heart on my wedding day."

As if his heart had ever been at risk.

Still, the romantic in Christine wasn't about to rain on the bride's parade. Planting a kiss on her new friend's cheek, she made sure she didn't leave a lipstick print before backing away.

"You have my solemn promise that won't happen."

"Good. Now will you go find my big brother for me and tell him to get his cute butt out here so he can give me away? I've got a man to marry!"

Her words met with whoops of approval inside the limo while Christine quietly hyperventilated. Giselle wanted her to find Vito?

So much for her elaborate plans to avoid him. It looked as though she had no choice but to face the man she'd fallen in love with against all better judgment.

Running up the church steps, she could hear the organ music playing right through the heavy wooden doors kept shut in deference to the air-conditioning on the warm Florida afternoon. She reached for one of the doors just as another swung wide.

Revealing the very person she'd been looking for.

She froze, drinking in the sight of Vito after the days they'd spent apart. What was it about a tuxedo that made a woman's heart pound? Her mouth go dry? Her hormones surge?

Oh, who was she kidding? It wasn't the tuxedo. It was most definitely the man inside it—even if he had no respect for her independence as a business professional and zero regard for her heart.

"Giselle sent me to look for you." She blurted as soon as her tongue came unstuck from the roof of her mouth. "She's ready for you to escort her—"

Her words died in her throat as he stalked closer. Closer.

Hauled her into his arms and planted a kiss on her lips that made her toes curls and her knees melt.

"Thank you for being here." He reached for the church door with one hand, never taking his hazel eyes off her. One of Vito's brother's peered out of the church, dressed just like him. "My brother will show you where to sit so I can find you afterward, okay? We need to talk."

He sounded so sincere, his dark eyes earnest. She knew she couldn't afford to get caught up in the romance of the day. The tuxedo. The church. The wedding music.

"Yes, we do." She struggled to remember the guilt

money he'd given her before he left on his trip. She needed to give it back to him anyway, so there was really no use avoiding him any longer. "I'll see you inside."

He might have said more, but the bridal party chose that moment to spill out of the limo, their laughter carrying on the breeze along with strains of "The Way You Look Tonight."

Sliding out of his arms, she ducked inside the church while her inner romantic prepared for the emotional roller-coaster ride of a wedding ceremony on the same day she'd be saying goodbye to Vito forever.

Good thing she'd brought along her hankie.

VITO KNEW it was a good thing he'd put Nico and Renzo in charge of making sure Christine got to the reception or she would have bolted the moment the church bells rang after Giselle's wedding.

Something was obviously bothering her or she wouldn't have made such a concerted effort to avoid him all day.

Now, an hour after his sister had said "I do," a string quartet played in the backyard during cocktails, and Vito scanned the grounds to find Christine. The family photos had taken forever, but he could hardly complain since his baby sister would only have one wedding day. While the bride continued to pose for photos with her groom and her girlfriends, Vito searched every section of the yard for signs of his garden goddess, not an easy task with one hundred and fifty of their closest friends and family on the scene.

He was just about to head in the house to check indoors when he remembered the tire swing. Hidden behind one of the minibars erected for the event, the old tire remained empty. But sure enough, there she was a few feet away, checking out the progress of the thatch palms they'd pruned together.

She looked beautiful in a long yellow dress with delicate daisies stitched across the hem, her silky dark hair curling around her ears. She seemed so much a part of the gentle floral landscape she'd designed out of the long-ignored yard. Vito couldn't picture this place without her in it.

"There you are." He hadn't realized he'd spoken until she turned the full impact of her bright blue eyes on him.

"Here I am." She spoke softly, as if she was already far away from him. Her fingers flexed around a tall, skinny glass, empty except for some ice. "The wedding was beautiful, Vito, but I can't stay for long."

"Can't stay?" Something was really wrong here. Drastically, incredibly wrong and he had no clue what. "Come on, Christine. You promised to be my date tonight and I've been saving up things that I need to tell you for five whole days. I've just got a few more commitments to Giselle since I'm the stand-in father of the bride for the day, but then we need to talk about what happens from here."

"Nothing happens from here." She reached inside a white purse tucked under one arm and withdrew a long white envelope. "We both knew that fling was finite when we got into this in the first place, so there's no need to pretend we're heartbroken now that summer is ending." Thrusting the envelope into his hands, she cleared her throat. "This is the extra money you inadvertently gave me when you paid for the landscaping job, so I'll hand that back to you now and call us even with no hard feelings."

It's a damn good thing the tire swing was behind him to catch him when he fell because Vito knew he'd keel over from shock any minute.

"You're saying it's over, you're leaving, and that the fling was finite...and you expect there to be no hard feelings?" He shook his head, refusing to believe his ears. "Weren't you in the same bed as me five days ago when we connected on some kind of superhuman level? And you know damn well I'm not just talking about the sex."

She peered meaningfully around the yard as if to remind him of his hundred and fifty wedding guests.

As if they mattered more than her right now.

She waved the envelope under his nose again before stuffing it in his jacket pocket.

"You're the one who set the ground rules for this relationship, not me." She sounded angry. Frustrated. Hurt. "And you're also the one trying to mix business with pleasure by ridiculously overpaying me for my skills. I wanted to be paid for professional assets and not my ass, remember?"

Now it was Vito's turn to peer around the yard and make sure no one could overhear them. Thankfully, even the string quartet was difficult to hear in a crowd of excited Italians snapping pictures and critiquing the passed hors d'oeuvres.

"You're mad about the bonus?" He'd given her some extra money when he had paid her. Had it been too much? Hell, he couldn't even remember the amount. "I saw how hard you worked this summer. Days, nights, weekends. Other people get time and a half for that kind of commitment, Christine."

"I didn't sign on for special treatment because I slept with the boss, okay? I don't need anyone to take care of me." Christine clutched her empty lemonade glass tighter and wished she hadn't guzzled it all down at once. She needed something to do to cool off the hot hurt inside her, needed an action to keep her nervous hands occupied, since just looking at Vito made her want to throw herself in his arms. Feel his hands all over her.

"*That's* what this is about?" He scratched his head, clearly perplexed that she'd be so mad about the money. "Hell, I thought you were upset because I took off for Germany so fast the other day."

She rattled the ice in her glass, sipped the few drops of water it yielded. Stalled until she could respond to that without sounding like all the other women in his life who'd ever tried to cling to him with both hands.

"I've understood from the beginning that you have a whole life outside me." Which was why she needed to leave this noisy, wonderful family shindig before she thought too much about what it would be like to be a part of that life.

The string quartet's music came to a halt as a local rock band took the stage along one side of the lawn. Vito's brother Nico took up the microphone, his deep voice rumbling over a squeaky hiss of electronic feedback. "Paging brother of the bride, Vito Cesare."

Vito pulled her close, his hands wrapping around her waist as he whispered in her ear. "My life outside of you is now officially over."

Before she could process what that might mean, he squeezed her hand and tugged her into the thick of the crowd toward the stage. "But for right now, I've got to play surrogate father of the bride and I need you beside me."

Having no clue what else to do, Christine closed her eyes and held on.

SHE WOULD have had a blast at Giselle's reception if she hadn't been half scared of the future and half hopeful. Every time she caught Vito staring at her during dinner, she felt a mixture of thrill and hope, followed by dread that she was misinterpreting everything.

But the evening included all the things that made her

romantic heart beat faster. First, there had been a surprisingly sentimental toast to the bride and groom from Nico. Then Vito had decided they needed a photo of all the kids attending the wedding, so he took it upon himself to gather them all around the tire swing to capture the moment. Later, there had been lots of clinking of silverware on glasses and in turn, lots of long kisses between a glowing bride and a husband who couldn't have looked any more proud.

Now, as dinner finally wound down, the dancing began under a canopy of stars and a temporary pavilion of white lights. Vito and Christine's table was vacated as the other three couples seated with them got up to dance.

Across the yard, half the reception crowd was doing the Stroll while the band turned up the volume. Not that it mattered since the whole neighborhood seemed to be in attendance tonight. Mrs. Kowolski and Giuseppe Donzinetti were sneaking kisses a few tables away, the stars in their eyes even more obvious than the ones overhead.

"I thought I'd never get you alone." Vito's voice cut into her thoughts, pulling her attention away from all the people around them who seemed to have found their lifelong happiness.

"You call this alone?" She couldn't help but smile at the hundred and fifty guests crowding the yard.

"It's about as alone as you ever get when you come from a big family." He reached across the white linen tablecloth and covered her hand with his. "Except for the nights."

His gaze brought back the butterflies. The worries. The desire for him that she knew would never, ever go away.

"It was definitely a lot quieter earlier this summer." The warm night air brought back so memories of being out here with him. She thought about the nights in the outdoor shower. The encounters on the living-room floor. The dining room table. It had all been so private. So decadent. "But this is fun, too."

"I'm sorry about the money." His thumb traced soft circles over the back of her hand. Reminded her how much he knew about touching. Kissing. "I can see your point about overtipping and sending the wrong message, but I swear I was only thinking how damn hard you worked all summer. Giuseppe wasn't here to see how you got up in the middle of the night to water the grass before the sprinkler system went in. He didn't know how you fell asleep outside that night you were so exhausted from working all day."

His words touched her. Went a long way toward soothing her wounded pride.

"I thought maybe you were just throwing money at me to make me go away quietly." But she should have known him better than that. She *did* know him better than that, but she'd been too upset about the end of the fling and falling in love to really think through the money issue. "I guess I've been expecting the worst from men ever since the whole Rafe ordeal and that's not fair to you."

He scooped up her other hand as a conga line danced past their table, Vito's aunts and uncles all making smoochy faces at them as if to encourage kissing.

God, they were too much.

"I don't want you to go away quietly, Christine. As the matter of fact, I don't want you to go away at all, and that's what I've been trying to tell you all day." His pant leg brushed up against her lightweight yellow dress, eliciting a shiver over her skin.

Hope surged through her again, stronger and scarier than the little twinges she'd felt earlier that evening.

"What about the fling?" There would be no misunderstandings this time. No embarrassing confusion about what a man wanted from her.

"The fling is over and while it was a hell of a lot of fun, I don't ever want another one. I want you. For real. Forever."

A pathetic little yelp-squeal escaped her throat even though she knew he couldn't come close to backing up that statement. "But you have a career overseas. A whole life beyond Miami and me—"

"I'm done." He threaded his fingers through her hair cupping the back of her neck. "That's why it took me so long to get back here this week. I told my publicist to cancel the rest of my schedule this season, because whether you say yes or no, I'm finally ready to come back home. Back to my family. Back to where I'm meant to be."

"You quit racing?" She knew the thumping bass from the band must be confusing her ears because she couldn't have possibly heard that correctly. "And what do you mean, 'whether I say yes or no'?"

She'd heard that part right.

Vito maneuvered something in his hands, his fingers twisting a thick silver band off his pinky.

"I mean whether or not you decide to marry into this rowdy clan of mine." He reached for her hand and dropped the weighty band into her palm. "I can't ask you officially today since it's my sister's wedding and I don't want your day to be overshadowed by hers. But this ring is my promise to you that I will do this the right way and replace that band with the real deal if you'll have dinner with me one night this week."

Shock mingled with disbelief. And a whole lot of hope. Happiness. Her fist curled around the silver pinky ring still warm from his skin.

"You would really give up your whole racing career? All the glitz? The insane amount of money?" Even as she thought he was the most wonderful man on earth, she also feared maybe he'd lost his mind. "You'd turn your back on all that to come to Miami and marry a messy landscaper with no sense of style and skin that will wrinkle prematurely thanks to all that sun exposure, and—"

"Don't you dare try to talk me out of it." He pulled her chair closer to his, sitting so close his thighs bracketed hers at the table. "As long as you're protecting your health with lots of SPF, I think you'll look great in wrinkles. And frankly, I've been more of a family guy than a jet-setter most of my life. I think I was just waiting for the right incentive to come back home."

She gulped back the lump in her throat.

"Me?" She opened her palm to stare down at the heavy ring he'd given her.

"Yes." Leaning forward he brushed a featherlight kiss over her mouth. "You. I love you, Christine."

Twining her arms around his neck, she draped herself across him, flung herself into him the way she'd wanted to from the moment she'd spied him in his tuxedo today.

"I can't believe it. You never gave me so much as a clue." She squeezed tighter, a gurgle of teary laughter escaping her lips. "I love you, too, Vito. And I can give you very good assurances that if you want to take me out for dinner this week, the answer will be a highly affirmative, all-systems-go yes."

His hands slid around her waist, smoothed over her back as he held her to him. She could almost feel their heartbeats settle into an easy rhythm, a compatible tune that would echo in her ears long after the noise of the rock band faded away.

"And as for me giving up the insane amounts of

money, I wouldn't be so sure about that." His breath was warm against her ear as he spoke.

Leaning away from him, she peered up into his eyes, confused. "What do you mean?"

"You know how I spent so many hours on the computer this summer?" Trailing one finger down the strap of her dress, he favored her with a conspiratorial smile. "Part of the reason was because I wanted an excuse to spend more time around the house so I could be close to you. But my other reason was that I've been creating software for a commercial racing game and a system to let players design their own racetrack."

"Are you telling me that behind the Ferrari exterior beats the heart of a techno-geek?" She straightened his tie, smoothed a hand over his tuxedo jacket to savor the muscles beneath. "No wonder you were so helpful when I was having trouble with that digital sprinkler system."

"Hey, don't knock the nerd. This geek just licensed the rights to his first mass-produced computer game." He sounded genuinely excited. Happy.

"That's wonderful." She kissed his cheek to appease Uncle Giuseppe and Mary Jo who were making more smoochy faces two tables away. "I'm so happy for you."

"I've got a brand-new career that will ensure I don't ever have to make cabinets for a living again. And since I'll be loafing around the house while I work, I can probably venture out to some of your job sites just in case you need a hand during your first year in business." He straightened. "Assuming that doesn't tread on the whole independence thing you've got going."

"Hell, no." She pointed a finger at him. "I've seen you with pruning shears, Cesare. You could make yourself very useful at All Natural if you know how to take orders from a woman."

His gaze narrowed as he stared at her in the glow of the tiny white lights that decorated most of the yard now that night had long since fallen.

"I don't know how I'll do with that. Why don't we have a test run tonight after everyone else leaves? You can give me a few orders in the outdoor shower and see how I perform?"

She shivered in anticipation. Running her fingertips discreetly up his thigh, she whispered, "You've got yourself a deal. Now, what do you say we join everyone else on the dance floor?"

Vito's mouth slanted over hers, tasting her with a thoroughness that left her breathless. "It would be my pleasure to dance with you."

Christine followed him toward the pavilion lit up like a southern Christmas. The band switched tempo from a rock and roll beat to a more traditional Italian dance. As Vito's million and one relatives formed a circle holding hands, the bride left a space beside her for them.

They danced until they were hot and thirsty and laughing so hard Christine's belly hurt. And when Vito called for champagne all around to make one last toast to the bride and groom, his eyes never left hers.

Clinking her glass to his, she knew exactly which bride and groom he meant.

* * * * *

Joanne Rock returns to Harlequin Historical!
Look for her latest offering,
THE KNIGHT'S REDEMPTION,
coming in September 2004.

If you enjoyed what you just read,
then we've got an offer you can't resist!

Take 2 bestselling
love stories FREE!
Plus get a FREE surprise gift!

Clip this page and mail it to Harlequin Reader Service®

YES! Please send me 2 free Harlequin Temptation® novels and my free surprise gift. After receiving them, if I don't wish to receive anymore, I can return the shipping statement marked cancel. If I don't cancel, I will receive 4 brand-new novels each month, before they're available in stores. In the U.S.A., bill me at the bargain price of $3.80 plus 25¢ shipping and handling per book and applicable sales tax, if any*. In Canada, bill me at the bargain price of $4.47 plus 25¢ shipping and handling per book and applicable taxes**. That's the complete price and a savings of 10% off the cover prices—what a great deal! I understand that accepting the 2 free books and gift places me under no obligation ever to buy any books. I can always return a shipment and cancel at any time. Even if I never buy another book from Harlequin, the 2 free books and gift are mine to keep forever.

142 HDN DZ7U
342 HDN DZ7V

Name	(PLEASE PRINT)	
Address	Apt.#	
City	State/Prov.	Zip/Postal Code

* Terms and prices subject to change without notice. Sales tax applicable in N.Y.
** Canadian residents will be charged applicable provincial taxes and GST.
  All orders subject to approval. Offer limited to one per household and not valid to
  current Harlequin Temptation® subscribers.
  ® are registered trademarks owned and used by the trademark owner and or its licensee.

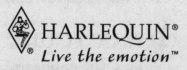

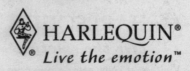